SPEECHLESS

Fated Mates – Book Three

Lilli Carlisle

ALSO BY LILLI CARLISLE

FATED MATES

Tigress

Huntress

THE BLACK RIDGE WOLF PACK

Omega's Choice

Ceva's Chance

Karli's Resolve

Laura's Legacy

Lili's Trust

Katrina's Destiny

www.BOROUGHSPUBLISHINGGROUP.com

SPEECHLESS
Copyright © 2019 LILLI CARLISLE

ISBN 978-1-951055-44-8

This has been possible only with the love and support of my family.
Love you Craig, Samantha, Katie, and Jason.

SPEECHLESS

Prologue

The nauseating scent of burning fur jolted Zahra from her sleep. She found herself beside her parents' graves in her old pack's territory in her wolf form. What she saw could not be possible. Instead of the remains of the former buildings, she found each in perfect condition, the same as she remembered them. Then, in an instant, the world around her burst into flames. Hunters ran with their guns at the ready, shooting any shifter in their paths, even unarmed women and children who were cowering on the ground.

Zahra tried to run to help them, but her body wouldn't move. She was held to the spot by some invisible hand and forced to watch as innocent people were gunned down like animals. She guessed it wasn't a far cry from their version of the truth, considering the human hunters saw them as such. Why couldn't the humans accept them, and their differences? It was fortunate that not many humans knew of their existence in this day and age. Now they were relegated to myth and folklore.

Each strangled cry and scream stabbed at her as the flames licked at her fur. She continued to struggle until all sound stopped, and the area fell silent. The flames were extinguished, leaving her in the inky dark. Thankfully, her eyesight was accustomed to the darkness, and she watched as every last hunter disappeared into the mist.

Bodies lay strewn across the long grass of her home. Her wolf whined before collapsing onto the dirt covering her parents and curling up into a ball, willing the images to leave her in peace. It had been over five decades since that had happened, and she relived it day after day, as if a blade was slashing at her throat over and over again. It all repeated in her mind, an endless loop of pain and suffering.

She wanted to run from the memories, fight something, anything, to get her pain out. But there was nothing left for her to fight over.

Zahra opened her eyes and stared at her mom and dad's little gravestones. She had managed to scratch and bite the rocks until their names were clear. Zahra would not forget them. The world may have kept on going around her, but she remained by their sides. Protecting all she had left and hoping death would come for her soon.

Chapter One

Zahra couldn't help but wonder if the Fates were toying with her again. As the sole survivor of her people, her pack, she relived the raid and extermination every day like a curse, as if she'd somehow forgotten the devastation that clawed at her throat night and day. For fifty years she'd remained as wolf, guarding her parents' graves, keeping a meager flame of remembrance burning in her heart, their memory the only will to live she had left.

When, unannounced and unexpected, the Porda Bear Clan had shown up and began excavating the area, she had hoped her prayers for death had been answered. They were searching for a gravesite on behalf of their matriarch, Rose. Zahra had watched the initial group survey the area for days while remaining a safe distance away, ensuring that the bear shifters stayed far from her parents. Though none appeared threatening, she had to stay alert.

More arrived. They'd expanded their search and were getting dangerously close to the graves Zahra swore to protect. One particularly large bear forced her to act when he dared to touch her mom's stone marker. Without any other choice, Zahra charged out of the cover of the forest at him, teeth and claws at the ready.

Then the fates went one step too far. A second bear came charging out in all his furry glory to protect her from the first bear, snarling and snapping, guarding her like she belonged to him. She had no idea what he was about, until he'd stayed by her side, and didn't leave even after his clan had left the area. Slowly, as she'd begun to trust him, she realized somehow, he was her fated mate. The general of the Porda Clan, a man named John. Whatever she'd done to deserve this kind of torment must have been horrendous, if she could only remember what that was.

Through this ordeal, Zahra had been reunited with her friend Rose, who was among the clan, and, unbelievably, was their matriarch. It had been well over fifty years since she'd seen Rose, the last time being when her friend was taken away from their birth pack to the safety of the North Woods Pack.

The bear shifters had been searching for Rose's parents' graves. Zahra knew exactly where they'd been buried, having witnessed the decimation the former alpha wolf triad had wrought, including killing her and Rose's parents. The triad had gone insane shortly before the hunters came and burned the village down.

During their reunion, a group of collector demons had pierced the veil between their realms and were intent on wiping out the clan. The evil creatures had been banished centuries earlier, but over time, they grew strong once again and had returned.

Zahra had arrived on Porda Clan land late last night, even though everyone else had returned days ago. She hadn't wanted to leave her parents behind after watching over them for so many decades. John had stayed with her as Zahra tried to reason with her wolf that she could come back and visit whenever she wanted. Her parents were safe now that the Porda Clan owned the land and marked the gravesites. Fences were going up, and proper gravestones were made to mark each of the sites where a body was found.

She'd gone with John only after they had agreed that if this new life didn't work out, she would hightail it back to what was left of her former village. She had been on her own for a long time, returning would be easy, except for having to leave John behind. But, while they might be mates, she wasn't certain she wanted to seal the deal. The idea of being tied to another being for eternity was daunting in the best of circumstances. Zahra was wolf, and John, a bear. She was an outsider in his world, and had been alone too long to hitch herself to someone else's future. And, regardless of Rose's status as matriarch, Zahra doubted she'd ever feel comfortable among a clan of bears.

The General of the warriors had been hard to shake. It wasn't until the alpha triad had promised her a room, which no one could enter without invitation, that Zahra had been able to think clearly. Having a fated mate had never crossed her mind. Learning that evil beings called collector demons were able to breach the separation between two realms was a revelation she could've done without. Living with bears was almost beyond her comprehension. She needed time to come to terms with it all, and the sizeable bear hovering over her wasn't helping.

True, Zahra felt a pull to the kind and handsome man. John had been patient, but she didn't understand why he was hers. She wasn't an alpha and didn't deserve a fated mate. Leaders alone retained that right. The bond would solidify a triad's ability to lead a pack, clan, or whatever the shifter group was called. She couldn't even contemplate what she'd do if a third showed up.

Zahra was left feeling out of control and floundering.

Now, she padded around her room, taking in the different scents of her new home. Everything was strange and unique. She felt as fearful as she was curious. Her pack had not associated with any others in all the years she'd been alive. The alpha triad had been in contact with other shifters when necessary, but the average pack member never had that power to seek them out even if they wanted to.

Their village had been modest and small compared to what she'd witnessed when arriving onto the Porda Clan's territory. Her entire home could have fit into this one room she'd been given.

Why do I feel so guilty about that?

Though her former alpha triad had a truck, electricity, and running water from a private well, the rest of the pack did without such luxuries. She remembered all the buckets of water she'd carried from the stream for her mom to cook or clean with and for bathwater.

Here there was a whole room dedicated to washing in Zahra's *suite,* as Rose had called it. The tub was magnificent. The modifications done to the house made it easy to carry on living in her wolf form. From buttons on the floors that opened the doors to handles that Zahra could turn with her teeth. She had to admit to loving soaking in that considerable tub. The water was warm, not like the stream, and the entire room smelled like a field of flowers. She wondered where the actual flowers were.

Everywhere she looked, there was shiny metal and sparkling glass. The knobs they called taps shone under the bright lights. There were glass walls, and white stone veined with gray lines everywhere. When Zahra had stepped on the smooth stone, she'd expected it to feel cold on the pads of her paws but was surprised by its warmth. The mirrors didn't have a single crack, and, shockingly, had designs etched into them that looked like vines flowing around the edges with the occasional flower mixed in.

One of the only pieces that she hadn't been able to identify was a large square metal thing with tiny holes in it, coming out of the ceiling above the tub. She kept waiting for it to do something, anything. The thing had to be a light of some sort, however, the object never moved or lit up. She'd keep her distance from it for now.

In her room proper, there were three large wooden dressers along with a big mirror that went all the way to the ground. Zahra was having a hard time believing anyone would own enough clothing to fill all the drawers. The bed was as long as it was wide: seriously massive. When she jumped onto the mattress to lie down, Zahra, felt lost and left out in the open, vulnerable to attack. So she'd pulled the blanket off the bed and made herself a den in the closet. No one could sneak up on her that way, and she'd have a fighting chance if intruders came.

There was also something rectangular in shape, which sat on a pedestal on top of one of the dressers and showed images of strange places and people. *Did those people realize they were being watched?* She'd felt bad about watching them and asked Rose to turn it off. Zahra wanted to give those people their privacy, something she'd been denied living among her old pack.

From her windows she could see a whole village behind the clan house. The pristine houses had flowers planted in boxes hanging from the windows and wide lanes running between them. Every shifter she'd met had been friendly, and food was in ample supply in her room.

Actually, there was too much food. Zahra hadn't eaten so well in her entire existence. She assumed the clan must have mighty bears to be able to catch so much wild prey to sustain this large of a group of shifters.

For decades, Zahra had existed on what she could find. The occasional squirrel or, when she was fortunate, a fat rabbit. Nothing like what had been offered to her so far. She couldn't help but wonder if all this plenty was typical here in the outside world, and if so, why hadn't her alpha triad wanted to be part of it?

The position of the sun indicated it was midafternoon, and she had yet to leave her private space. No one had bothered her. Only a woman named Marie came regularly with food. She seemed friendly and talked a lot about the clan as Zahra ate.

The stories the bear shared were wondrous and scary. Marie had admitted to challenging Rose for the position of matriarch to the clan. After hearing the full story, Zahra understood Marie had been acting out of fear and self-preservation. Now the woman carried great shame for her actions like a heavy cloak across her shoulders.

Unfortunately, the longer Zahra stayed in her room, the more worked up she was getting. Would she fit in here? Did she want to? Would she anger people for not shifting into her human form? Would they grow tired of her lacking basic knowledge of the world? Did they want another wolf around?

Questions and concerns became imperatives and fear as scenarios of social disaster played out in her head. Always in the back of her mind was her return to the forest, whether from the slightest provocation or the humiliation of not fitting in. She existed on a knife's edge: lean too far one way or the other, and her life was over.

The thought of returning to her forest calmed her wolf. Having an escape plan had been driven into her for as long as she could remember. Her mom and dad had ensured they always had one, except for that last time when no one got out alive except her.

Zahra was starting to realize it was past time for her to explore her possible future. If she elected to stay here, she had to get out of this room. All those decades mourning at her parents' graves didn't change what had happened to her family and her pack. If lying down and dying beside her parents was not an option, and clearly it wasn't since she'd kept herself alive for over fifty years, then she had to get on with life, whatever that looked like. Admitting she was scared right down to the marrow in her bones had her hesitating, but it didn't stop her. She padded over to the door and pushed the open button on the floor with her paw. As the door opened, she worried there would be people waiting for her, but she found the hallway was empty.

Zahra knew her room was in the clan house reserved for the alpha triad and presumed not all clan members had access, which eased her worry. So far, the only person she could have a conversation with was Rose since she'd been part of Zahra's old pack. She had no ability to reach members of the Porda Clan's minds. They didn't share the same blood. As for John, initially, she hadn't wanted to share blood with him. Now, she wasn't sure she wanted to take that step to solidify a bond that was eternal.

Here, she was an outsider in a clan full of bears. How she had thought this would be a good idea was a testament to her unbalanced state. Since she'd arrived on Porda lands, she'd had a low ringing in her head that she'd attributed to stress, but its constant din portended bad things, and she'd had enough bad to last ten lifetimes.

Zahra walked to the main door, the one that led to the rest of the house and the clan. John was never far from her thoughts, and she wondered where the big bear was. She didn't want to *be* with him, but she wouldn't mind seeing him. Things were so messed up right now, and her emotions were all over the place. She held a lot of guilt for putting the man through this.

Taking a deep breath, she pressed the button to open the main doors. She had to give this an honest shot, or she indeed was the *nothing* her old triad had told her to be.

Directly in front of the doors stood two towering bear shifters. Rose had told her that they were posted here to protect her, and the alpha triad, but Zahra wasn't so sure. In her pack, the biggest often would take advantage of the smaller wolves.

When neither of the warriors moved toward her, Zahra steeled her nerve and padded forward into what appeared to be an expansive communal space. Her old pack didn't bother with such areas. Most stayed to themselves and hoped to go unnoticed by the triad.

Deep couches and large chairs sat throughout the room while leaving space for the clan to amble by in their bear forms. Stone fireplaces stood on either end of the room, surrounded with large area rugs and sizeable cushions scattered on the floor, welcoming people to come and lie down.

The warmth and invitation the surrounding presented made Zahra more guarded. If she got used to these comforts, it could lead to her downfall. Prosperity was foreign to her, and it seemed as though the bears chose comfort as a way to express theirs. She imagined they worked hard for what they had, which made her question her worth. What exactly was she bringing to the table?

What she'd encountered here had been what Zahra had dreamed of all her life: a home, food, love, comfort, and safety. However, now that this dream was becoming a reality, she wasn't sure if she wanted it. All the excess felt unnatural, even though she felt certain no one in the Porda Clan saw these creature comforts as excessive.

"I see you've come out of hiding," a soft voice said from behind Zahra.

She spun around so quickly that her claws became caught up on a small area rug she'd been standing on, causing her to tumble onto her side. She couldn't help her slight yelp when she hit the hardwood floor, which made her angry with herself for being caught out. She couldn't show any weakness, especially now, when surrounded by strangers. However, she didn't have enough padding between her skin and bone to cushion the fall. She heard the slight crack on impact.

The roar of rage that followed was even more surprising. *Shitty-shit-shit-shit.*

Before she had a chance to right herself, John, followed by the alpha triad, came charging into the room. Her friend, Rose, the matriarch, pushed past her mates and asked, "What happened?"

Zahra's would-be mate didn't stop to ask questions before lifting her into his arms and causing her to yelp again in pain. *Great. All I wanted to do was take a look around unnoticed. Now everyone is staring at me.*

"You're hurt," John growled before staring daggers at Marie, who'd gone quiet. The threat of violence sat thick in the air. Their animal halves were fighting for control. Physical altercations were frequent among shifters when their animals got involved. Zahra had to stop this from escalating, or there could be some big-ass bears batting each other around.

"She didn't hurt me. I fell." The ringing in her ears was getting worse as an argument erupted. No one had heard Zahra, and more warriors were arriving, obviously alerted by their General's anger. Things were getting out of hand fast.

Zahra concentrated as hard as she could and yelled, *"Stop."* To her relief, all the growling ceased, and blessed silence reigned. She was used to silence. Silence was good. Even the ringing in her ears had disappeared. She'd been alone for so long that shouting and excessive noise made her fur stand on end. The only problem: now everyone was silently staring at her as if she'd grown another head.

Zahra rubbed her muzzle with her paw to confirm that wasn't the case. There had been a lot of crazy shit happening around here lately.

"I heard you," John said. His gaze softened when he looked down at her, still tucked in his arms. "Somehow, you made the connection into the clan link on your own."

"We all heard you. How is that possible?" Riker asked as he gathered Rose into his arms. "It wasn't a connection through mates, but with everyone."

"I imagine the same way I was able to access the clan connection before we mated," Rose said. "Though Zahra has done it at an accelerated rate." Rose looked proud of her, but Zahra wasn't so sure that it was a good thing. She'd been alone in her mind for decades, and now the once trickle of awareness she had of the clan was blown wide open into a raging river.

However, above anything else, she had to make sure they knew the truth of what happened. *"Marie didn't hurt me, my claws caught on the rug, and I fell."* Zahra wouldn't allow Marie to take the fall for this. She laughed at her own pun, fall—fall.

"After I scared you. I should never have come up behind you like that," Marie was quick to admit, accepting the blame when she shouldn't.

"Marie, it's not your fault that I'm a bit jumpy. Until I become more familiar with the clan, I'm afraid a stray wind would have had the same effect on me. I've been alone for a long time. It will take me a bit of time to get used to so many shifters in one place."

Marie nodded, but Zahra wasn't buying it. She'd have to have a private talk with her once they had a chance because she doubted John would let her out of his sight any time soon.

"We'll have Jewel take a look at you," John insisted. Zahra didn't even try to fight the decision, knowing it would be the only way to calm her mate down.

A multitude of voices poured through her link, welcoming her to the clan. Thankfully, Zahra had learned how to control her thoughts from years living under her old alpha matriarch's rule. As Zahra was carried to an infirmary of some sort, she spread her thanks to the clan.

Nothing in her own healer training prepared her for the weird-looking machines of some sort along the walls. Zahra had learned the ancient arts of healing from her mother, and they included nothing like this. When John laid her down on a small bed, a bright light switched on above her. Zahra was temporarily blinded, and, of course, she freaked out.

The second she'd moved to jump from the bed, she found herself in her mate's arms and was engulfed in a sense of peace she'd never known. Someone turned the light away, but instead of releasing her to lie back down, John lay on the bed beside her.

Okay, get yourself together. My parents didn't raise a coward.

"You are far from being a coward," John whispered into her fur at the back of her neck. The move sent chills down her spine and started fires in other places. "You are one of the bravest people I know. You survived a brutal pack, annihilation, and survived on your own for decades. I see no cowardness in you, my mate."

She rubbed her muzzle against John's chest, which seemed to make the big guy happy. Through their link, he told her Jewel was a doctor and was sister to the alpha triad.

"So, what do we have here?" Jewel asked as she walked in.

For the first time since being laid on the bed, Zahra looked up and felt some of her anxiety slip away. John, Jewel, and Zahra were in the room, and no one else. Standing out and being the center of attention was what got her in trouble with her pack all those years ago, and they'd taken her voice as retribution.

"Zahra fell and hurt her fifth and sixth rib on her right side," John answered.

"How do you know what hurts? You didn't see me fall."

John smiled wide before stating, "I'm your mate. I can feel your pain. That's what brought me running in the first place."

"Is that normal between mates?"

"Actually, by how specific John was when sensing your pain, I'd say it is unique," Jewel answered as she took out a few instruments. The only one Zahra could identify was the stethoscope. "Alpha triads can often sense each other's pain but only in general terms. I've never heard of a similar case with such specifics."

"But we aren't a triad, and I'm not an alpha."

"No, you're not. Research has begun into our history to confirm if there has ever been another case like this or with any other shifters," Jewel explained before placing her small hand on Zahra's side. "You are special, Zahra, and completely accepted here among the Porda Clan."

"Yes, you are," John reiterated as he held her tighter to his chest before Jewel began examining her. Zahra was on edge and testy, especially since she was in pain. It was safer for him to hold her tight so that she didn't snap at the doctor. Once she accepted the clan, such safeguards would no longer be necessary, as the clan wouldn't be a threat to her, they would be family.

As Jewel pressed on her ribs, Zahra forced control over her natural reactions. She would not hurt one of the people who had been kind to her. John loosened his hold slightly and began talking about his day.

Zahra knew he was trying to distract her, but he didn't realize something Jewel had said was already keeping Zahra preoccupied. *Special.* Her mom had used that term for her, but she didn't see what they saw, and probably never would.

Chapter Two

John stood outside Zahra's bedroom door, waiting for her to answer. He'd never walk in on his mate before he'd gained permission. He would never ruin her sense of safety and self. Hell, John was still trying to figure out why the Gods chose him for such an honor as a fated mate. It wasn't as if he were alpha or even powerful. Sure, he'd spent his life in the service of the Porda Clan keeping everyone safe from harm, but that was his duty. There wasn't a single thing that made him different than any other bear shifter.

The click of the door opening captured his attention. There would be time enough to figure this out. John hoped that the Gods wouldn't realize their mistake and take her away from him. That would be a death sentence. Neither he nor his bear would survive without Zahra.

All he had seen was Zahra's wolf. And what a beauty she was: inky black with a white tuft at the end of her tail. John couldn't help but wonder if her hair would have a stripe of white when she was in human form.

"Are you ready for our walk around the property?"

John could feel her joy even before she spoke through their link. *"Yes."* Her wolf was almost bouncing with excitement.

He stepped back, allowing his mate to pad out into the hallway. He wasn't sure why she hadn't shifted back into her human form, but he wouldn't push her. She would do it when she was ready. He was happy to have her in his life in any way possible, and in whichever form she chose.

"I'll show you around our community behind the clan house and our brew houses, as well as a few places where the sun hits just right for a warm nap."

"You bears take your comfort seriously, don't you?" Zahra asked.

"You bet we do." John laughed. "Considering all that's coming our way, I'll take all the comfort I can get."

"You mean more collector demons?"

"Yes. It won't be long before those vipers make their move and the world as we know it will cease to exist. The clan is preparing for their arrival. You are safe here. We've taken in members of smaller shifter groups unable to defend themselves alone, a cast of hawks, and a clowder of ocelots." John didn't want his mate to feel anything but safe. "We've stockpiled weapons, medical supplies, food, gold, and silver. Below the clan territory, there are many subterranean levels where we will be safe if needed."

"Why gold and silver?"

"When everything goes to hell, the modern-day currency isn't going to be worth anything. Precious metals will hold value in trade for things we may need." John didn't want to keep a thing from his mate. Knowledge could save her life, and he'd do anything to protect her.

"Rose told me about the reincarnations of ancient goddesses from the time of the great war when shifter and human fought side by side to defeat these same demons. Do you think we'll be as fortunate this time around?" Zahra's voice took on a deeper tone.

"We have to be. We have no other choice, and humans have no idea what's headed for them. They've forgotten their past and buried it under myth and legend," John explained. "But enough of worrying over what might be. Let's go for that tour and maybe a run afterward if you're up to it."

"My ribs have healed, I'd love to." Zahra's voice returned to its normal happy tone. John wished it would stay this way but knew sooner or later they'd be facing those cruel creatures again.

John stepped outside onto the large stone back patio and began to strip. He didn't want to ruin any more clothing while shifting. He'd be forced to have to order new clothes again. Bear-sized men couldn't buy off the rack; their clothing had to be made. Nudity wasn't uncommon among shifters, even though his mate averted her gaze to give him privacy. Gods, she was adorable.

"Adorable? Pups and cubs are adorable, mister," Zahra growled. *"I'm all wolf, strong, powerful, and majestic. Not adorable."*

"Majestic?" His eyebrow rose in question.

"That's right, bear," Zahra teased, swiping her tail from side to side. *"Catch me if you can."*

Zahra took off like a bullet, heading straight for the forest. John couldn't contain his happiness at seeing his mate being comfortable enough to be playful. His roar vibrated off the brick walls behind him the second he shifted. Without any hesitation, John took off after his mate, not caring who saw the general of the warriors behaving like some hormonal teenager.

John had never taken a permanent mate, so he had some catching up to do.

***

Zahra had no idea what came over her. She'd never engaged in play, even when she was a child. In her pack, anything remotely viewed as wasting time was frowned upon. The children had to do their share of work for the pack. Now, she was running around Porda Clan territory with an eight-hundred-pound bear closing in on her without a care in the world. A strange juxtaposition.

For this one moment in time, she was free to feel the wind in her fur, and the joy of being alive. For that alone, Zahra would have given John the world if she could, further confirming her belief that she'd made the right decision coming here with him.

"I'm catching up, little wolf," he ribbed as he caught up to within a dozen feet of her.

"That's what you think," she replied as she dug her claws into the damp forest floor and pivoted to the left off a tree trunk before taking off at a ninety-degree angle. She heard the snapping of tree limbs as her mate skidded to a stop several feet past where she'd once been. *"All that extra weight does have its drawbacks."*

John's laughter floated across their link, making her even happier if that were possible. Up ahead, she could see a pond with a small dock jutting out from the shore and made a break for it. After so much running, she needed to cool down and wondered if the big bear would follow her in.

Without breaking stride, she ran over the worn wood of the dock and jumped headfirst into the cold water. She broke the surface in time to see her bear launching himself off the dock and splashing down several feet away from her. The waves he created had her bobbing around like a buoy and made her laugh even harder.

When John surfaced, he was back in his human form. His dark hair and skin seemed to shine even brighter in the sunlight. His muscular arms waved through the water, keeping him afloat while his sage green eyes locked on her.

"Did you think I wouldn't follow you in, little wolf?"

"Actually, I was a little worried you'd sink to the bottom."

He splashed her. "What happened to the quiet, shy wolf I met only weeks ago?"

"She's decided to trust you," she blurted.

John's face froze as if he'd been struck, and a few seconds later, he said, "I'm overjoyed to hear you say that. You have nothing to fear from the clan or me. I wish to care for you."

"I believe you."

Over the past several days, Zahra had been exploring farther from her room. She'd met an older woman named Joanne and her younger helper, Hope. Both had been friendly and kind, and neither made a big deal over the fact that Zahra remained in her wolf form. They acted as if it were a common occurrence. Who knew? Maybe it was.

"Besides, Rose would go all super-crazy-wolf on anyone who even looked at you the wrong way," he joked. "Not to mention having a pissed-off bear to deal with. Nobody wants that."

Zahra liked how her mate kept everything light and cheerful. She'd had enough darkness for one lifetime, thank you very much.

"It's good to have friends in high places." She swam over to a small beach, shook out her coat of thick fur, dispersing most of the water from her body and onto the sand.

John had followed her out and shifted back into his bear by the time Zahra had turned around. *"Come with me, I have something to show you,"* he said.

She and her mate ran back into the forest side by side. John's bear dwarfed her smaller wolf, but she wasn't afraid, as she'd been before around larger wolves. She knew it would take a long time for her to put the past behind her, if she ever could, but right here, in this moment with John, was the best way to start trying.

After about twenty minutes, he began to slow and eventually stopped on the edge of a small clearing. Her mouth dropped open.

She couldn't believe what she was seeing. The wide area was covered in pink honeysuckle, above a sea of ferns. Brilliant sunlight poured down on the clearing, giving the space an almost ethereal look.

"This is beautiful." Zahra wished she knew stronger words to describe what she was feeling. She drew in deep breaths of the fragrant air, lifting her spirits even higher.

"I thought you might like to rest for a while here, together." The big bear sounded unsure, and Zahra knew that was due to her past behavior. She may still be confused about the direction of her life, but she wasn't about him.

"That sounds wonderful," she eagerly agreed before stepping out into the clearing. The sun was warm on her fur and felt like a hug.

When they came to roughly the center of the area, John laid his big bear body down and rolled on the ground, creating a bed of ferns for them to lie on. Zahra joined him, rubbing her side against his as she curled up next to her bear as he chuffed in happiness.

It wasn't long before she heard his breathing evening out, giving her a chance to think long and hard about what she was considering doing. Out here in this stunning clearing, there was only the two of them. No one else would see her. It was wrong to hide away from her mate, but Zahra worried he would be disgusted by what he saw. She was every time she caught her reflection in the river back in her forest, one of the only other times she'd shifted since.

She'd never know if she didn't at least try once.

***

John would have purred if he'd been a cat shifter. The feel of delicate fingers carding through his fur felt terrific, making him stretch. This was by far the best way to wake up to his mate.

Fingers?

He opened his eyes, and sure enough, they were still in the clearing. Which could only mean one thing: Zahra had shifted into her human form. Slowly he shifted out of his bear form, not wanting to move too quickly and alarm her. When the warmth from the palm of her small hand pressed against his skin, he couldn't contain the moan of pleasure at having his mate finally touch him in this way. Skin to skin.

Zahra had yet to speak, but that didn't deter him one bit. With deliberate movements, he turned around to see his mate, face-to-face, for the first time.

"You're stunning, my mate," he whispered as he took in her long black hair, which, sure enough, had a streak of bright white running down from her left temple. Zahra's pale skin looked so soft that he had to stop himself from touching her. Deep blue eyes watched him closely in a sort of confusion.

"I'm not stunning," Zahra said through their link while running her hands over the multiple scars crisscrossing her throat.

John tamped down his anger at the thought of someone causing his mate so much pain. He moved a few inches closer and gently took one of her hands away from her throat. "These do not detract from your beauty, my mate. Nothing ever could."

"They took my voice." The sadness radiating off her was crushing.

John could feel her pain. "Who did, Zahra?"

"The Alpha Matriarch, once she'd discovered what I'd done," Zahra said in a soft voice, as if the ghosts of her past would hear her and attack.

"What could you have ever done to deserve this?" Nothing could account for this amount of cruelty. Then he was reminded of the pain and suffering Matriarch Rose had been put through at the hands of that psychotic triad. The three of them had been completely insane, not to mention finding out the matriarch had been infected by a collector demon. Considering this had occurred over fifty years ago, the matriarch's soul must have been black for such a weak demon to possess it so easily.

"I made her mates take Rose to safety," Zahra said matter-of-factly, confusing John even more.

"You were still young when Axel and Xander came from the North Woods Pack to save Rose. There's no way you could have forced them to do anything. Your old matriarch was without a doubt sadistic. None of this is your fault."

Zahra looked away for a moment, and John could feel her indecision and fear through their bond, but also a bit of hope. With a decisive nod of her head, she turned to face him once more. *"My mother called it the voice of the gods. All I knew was that if I concentrated hard enough on someone, I could make them do what I wanted with only my voice. The one and only time I used it was to convince the alpha and beta to contact an outside pack to take Rose away.*"

"Then, they took your voice." John was shocked. Rose's freedom came at more of a cost than any of them ever knew.

"*Yes, they tried at first. However, with shifter accelerated healing, the first attempt didn't take, or the second and third.*" Zahra stopped for a moment as if collecting her thoughts before continuing. "*I was muzzled and thrown into the same pit Rose had been released from. Eventually, over time and multiple attempts, they were able to silence me. That's the only reason I survived the hunters that day. I was in the covered pit when they attacked, and no one noticed me.*" Zahra let out a deep breath. Even though she hadn't spoken a word aloud, the emotional weight of it had to be the same.

Fury and rage warred inside him, but John knew there wasn't anyone left to pay for these crimes. His bear didn't see it the same way. "I would have done anything to spare you that pain, but I am thankful the hunters didn't find you."

"*At times, I've wished they had,*" Zahra began, wringing her hands together. "*Why would the gods have given me this gift only to allow others to take it away when I try to do good with it? They called me a freak, a nothing. What am I now?*"

John took her other hand in his and brought her palm to his lips for a kiss. His heart ached for what his mate had gone through. "I can't explain the will of the gods, Zahra, but I do know who and what you are. You are my kind, strong, and beautiful mate, who also happens to be a Siren of sorts."

"*Wait, don't they have scales and fins, along with a lust for killing sailors? My parents had old books they used to teach me to read.*" John loved the way her nose scrunched up when she was confused.

John gathered her into his arms and cocooned her against his body, thankful that she allowed him to. "The legend changes depending on who you ask. Ancient Greeks believed them to be half-woman, half-bird, while Romans linked them to the sea. Stories have been written about them since chisel first struck stone in ancient Egypt."

"*How do you know so much about this?*" she asked before cuddling closer to him.

"The study of shifter history has been a passion of mine for as long as I can remember. I'm a bit of an anthropologist and archaeologist rolled into one. I went as far as getting my doctoral degree in the study of anthropology even though it was centered around the study of human behavior and societies. I adapted it to our varied shifter histories." He had always been a bookworm. Even though he was a hulking bear general to his clan, he loved researching history.

"Wow, so does that make you a doctor?" she teased, and he understood she was trying to get past all the pain. It amazed him how much literal knowledge Zahra had from her parents' old books and how little real-world experience she had. *"Guess it no longer matters now that I have no voice. I can never use it again."*

"Absolutely everything about you matters. Never forget that." He held her closer to stress his point. "Maybe by explaining what happened to Rose and Raz, it will help them figure out what's going on."

"No. That will never happen. I would sooner return to my forest. I will not lay that guilt at Rose's feet. I made that choice alone, and alone I will live with it." Zahra's voice rang through their link with certainty.

John cupped the side of Zahra's face and tried not to concentrate on the fact that she threatened to leave. If she did, he would follow her to the ends of the earth. She would never be left to fend for herself again.

"You're not alone any longer, Zahra. I stand by your side, mate, no matter what comes our way." Slowly lowering his lips to hers, he couldn't wait to share the wonder of their first kiss. Her soft lips slid over his as they tested and tasted one another for the first time, knowing it would be far from their last.

Chapter Three

"What the hell do you mean you can't tell me?" Rose asked as she circled John, behaving like the predator she was. "I'm your matriarch. I can force you to tell me."

John chose his words carefully. "Yes, you can, Matriarch."

"Damn it, you know I won't, but I want answers," Rose said as she threw her hands up into the air.

"Yes, Matriarch. You would never force your will on anyone else." He couldn't help the small smile that crossed his lips. Rose was a fair and compassionate matriarch.

"Please tell me why Zahra won't see me." Rose seemed to deflate right in front of him, making both her mates growl at him in a warning.

John wished he could explain, but he'd sworn a promise to his mate that he'd keep her secret until she was ready to share it. The problem began when Zahra had not been able to shift back into her wolf form after the two of them had talked in the clearing. He had secreted her back into the clan house and her room after dark. No matter how hard or often she tried, she couldn't shift, leaving her stuck in human form and unable to hide her scars under layers of fur.

"Zahra needs more time before seeing anyone." That was the best he could do, and he knew the excuse sounded lame.

"More time? I saw her yesterday," Rose countered.

"For what?" Mason asked. "Is she unwell? Jewel can look at her immediately." A sense of urgency flooded the room.

"No, no, she's well." John could imagine the fuss getting the doc involved would cause.

When it looked like Riker was about to take up the cause, fear carrying through the link combined with a slamming door alerted the four of them to a disturbance not far from the office. John knew the only rooms this close to the office were in the alpha triad's private wing. *Shit. "Zahra?"*

When he didn't receive an answer, he took off at a run, knowing full well the alpha triad would be following close behind. He pushed past two of his warriors, who were now standing outside of Zahra's closed bedroom door alongside Hope, who had broken down into tears.

"I'm so sorry, I didn't know, and didn't mean to share it with the clan. I swear it," Hope cried. "I would have never taken the tray in, but I knocked, and when no one answered. I assumed Zahra was out."

John hadn't missed the tray of food now sitting on the floor in the hall or the way Hope held her right hand protectively against her neck. She'd caught Zahra unaware, scared the hell out of his mate, and seen her scars before sharing her shock with everyone.

This wasn't the way either of them wanted the clan to find out. But now it was too late. He needed to find and comfort his mate. He knocked on Zahra's bedroom door and waited, but received no response. He opened the door enough for him to slide his body through and to not allow others to look in, but his mate was nowhere to be seen.

John stepped inside the room and called out, "Zahra?"

"Please leave," she whispered through their private link.

"You know I can't leave you like this. You're my mate, and I love you." Okay, that last part slipped out, but it was the truth. Though he would have chosen a much different time and more romantic way to express it.

"You love me?"

"How could I not," he stated as he neared the closed ensuite door. "Your continued strength and compassion after everything you've been through is remarkable. Your loyalty to Rose and your parents decades after the pack was gone amazes me. And your wish to protect others, though I believe misguided in this case, only confirms that you're way too good for a lowly general whose best trait is training warriors. But I'll be damned if I'm going to give you up."

"You're not lowly, you're perfect." She was quick to defend him.

"Thank you. So are you, my mate," he said as he laid the palm of his hand against the polished wood. "Please open the door for me."

Thankfully, she didn't make him wait long. The knob began to turn, and the door opened. She stood a few feet away, wearing one of his navy blue t-shirts, which hung down to her knees. He liked what he saw. She looked good in his clothing. His bear agreed wholeheartedly. Covering Zahra in his scent brought out his baser instincts. But now was not the time to get caught up in those musings; his mate's gorgeous blue eyes were swimming with tears.

"Does the whole clan know now?" she asked.

John couldn't lie. "Hope wasn't able to shield her thoughts in time. It was an accident."

"I thought so when the link filled with shock. I blocked everyone out after that. Except for you," Zahra explained.

"Thank you. I'm not sure what I'd do if I couldn't sense and reach you." Though Zahra hadn't responded to his initial call, probably due to shock, he could still sense her in his mind.

Glancing back at the barely opened bedroom door, he sensed everyone had left except for a visibly shaken Rose. "You need to tell her what's going on."

Zahra took a deep breath and squared her shoulders. *"You're right."*

John held out his hand, and his mate quickly took it.

He hoped the two friends came out the other side of this nightmare whole.

***

Why am I behaving like a child? No. That's not right. I've known plenty of strong children. It all comes down to I never wanted Rose to see the truth. She's been through enough. I will always be a physical reminder of her painful past. What will happen if Rose can never look at me as a friend ever again?

Zahra held John's hand like a lifeline. She'd never wanted to do this. Having her secret revealed so suddenly was much worse than she could have imagined. To keep reminding Rose of that awful time was plain cruel, and to make her friend feel any guilt for what had happened made her want to run for her forest.

However, she was stuck in her human form. There was now a zero percent chance of working up to this confession because what she had fought to keep hidden stood out in the open for all to see.

Zahra's free hand came up to cover her throat time and time again, no matter how hard she tried to keep it down by her side. Each raised edge of flesh was achingly familiar, and still disgusted her. Rose stood in the middle of Zahra's bedroom, her mouth hanging open in silence.

"I'm sorry, Rose. I never wanted you to see this." Zahra put that out there right from the start. If there were any way to avoid this one moment, she would have done it.

Rose blinked her red-rimmed eyes a few times before closing her mouth and taking a seat on the edge of the bed. "Why? Who did this to you?"

Zahra felt her stomach churn as she came to sit down on the bed beside her friend before she collapsed. Decades of self-loathing and doubt slammed into her, and she was finding it hard to breathe. John's warm hand on her back soothed her when nothing else ever could. After a few long moments, Zahra's breathing returned to normal, and the pinholes of light left her vision.

"I'll leave the two of you to talk," John said as he released her hand. "I'll be outside if you need me."

Zahra nodded and watched as her generous mate left, shutting the door behind him. She and Rose were alone, but she was still at a loss for what to say. How would she even begin the sentence? *Um, remember back when you were in the pit?*

Rose must have felt Zahra's apprehension. She took the lead by asking a question to help get things going. "Is this the reason why you wouldn't shift to talk with John or me?"

"Yes. I no longer have a voice." That was a safe question. Straight to the point with no offer of additional information.

"Did the hunters do this to you when they attacked the pack?" Rose carried on, and Zahra could feel her stress pouring off her. The scent alone would bring other clan members to them with offers of assistance.

It would be so easy to go with that presumption. To blame those that hunted their kind. Even though the bastards were aware of shifters' human halves, they'd already killed and maimed so many. Trying as hard as she could, Zahra wouldn't lie to her old friend. *"No, it was the matriarch."*

Anger swept through the room unchecked, sharp, and deadly until Rose managed to get her emotions back under control.

"Why did she do this to you?" Rose's extended canines flashed as she spoke.

Here goes everything, ensuring that their relationship will never be the same between them ever again. *"The matriarch was furious when she found out that I made her mates release you."*

The confusion on Rose's face was to be expected, and Zahra knew what her next question would be before the words were given life. "What could the insane bitch have claimed you, a child, did to force her powerful mates to release me?"

With anger and confusion thick in the air, Zahra unwillingly opened her Pandora's box. *"I've been given a gift, or a curse, depending on what side of this you might be on. When I explained what happened to John, he mentioned that I might be some sort of Siren. Since I was a child, I knew I could make people do what I wanted them to do with my voice alone."*

Rose sat in stunned silence for several moments before her friend's eyes filled with tears. She reached for Zahra's hands and held them between her own as they shook uncontrollably. "You...you did that for me?"

"Of course. You had to get out of there. The matriarch would have killed you." Zahra remembered the escalating violence in those last few days. *"I listened as my mother kept saying for seasons that the triad had lost all sense of reality."*

"How did they discover it was you?" Rose asked, and Zahra couldn't miss the tears now streaming down her friend's face.

"I had never tried to use it on people before. I practiced on squirrels. Mom and Dad told me to hide what I was, knowing the triad would see me as a threat, but I couldn't put it off any longer." Zahra had no idea why, but the day she'd made a choice to use her power to free her friend, she'd been given a bone-deep feeling that it would be Rose's last day of life.

"Because I...I was near death." Rose's voice was much deeper now.

Zahra wasn't sure if that had been a question, but nodded anyway, though they both knew the truth. *"I was young and stupid. I didn't know how to hide my tracks. Once they'd done what I'd ordered them to do and you were safe, the spell wore off."*

"And they realized what you'd done."

Again, no answer was needed, but Zahra slowly nodded. *"I would have never used my power on anyone else, but they...they had it coming."* Zahra waved the index finger of her left hand toward her throat dismissively. *"It doesn't matter anymore; the gift is gone. This is all that's left of it."*

"Don't do that," Rose ordered, her voice brisk and short. "Don't try to diminish what you've been through or what you sacrificed to save me." She held out her hand for Zahra to take. "Please show me everything that happened after I was released."

Zahra pulled back her hands as far as she could so that Rose couldn't reach them. *"No. You don't want to see that. There's no need for specifics."*

"Please, I need to know," Rose pleaded. "If you're to carry this burden, I must carry it along with you."

Zahra hesitated and examined her pale hands as if they were snakes ready to strike. She understood Rose needed closure of some sort. Her old friend looked at her as if she had the power to clear up everything and somehow make sense of their joined pasts. But there could never be closure.

"You sure about this?" Zahra asked. She wouldn't be able to pick and choose what Rose saw if Zahra allowed her into those memories she fought to lock away long ago. Some of them she wished she wasn't forced to live with herself, let alone share.

"Yes." Rose smiled sadly. "I owe you my life. The least I can do is carry part of the load those memories place on you daily."

Decision made, she reached for Rose's hands before Zahra had a chance to change her mind. The moment their skin touched, decades of memories and nightmares flooded forward.

With her new abilities, Rose was able to delve into people's minds whether they opened a link or not. Rose had explained that she'd never done it without the person's permission. However, Zahra could see such a gift coming in handy as these collector demons gained in strength and numbers.

Scenes played out like a morbid nightmare filled with pain and violence. Though Zahra had tried to quiet the effect these memories were having on her, she couldn't stop them altogether. Her body shook with anxiety the longer she carried on.

Rose sat with her eyelids closed, taking it all in. A few times, Zahra felt her flinch, which only reinforced the guilt she was already feeling at having to put her friend through this. Growls could be heard coming from the other side of her closed bedroom door. Obviously, Rose's mates could feel her responses to what she was seeing.

The only other link left open belonged to Zahra's mate, and she believed it would have hurt John even more if she cut him out of what was happening. Grudgingly, she allowed him to join this screwed-up walk down memory lane. From the day Rose was taken to safety away from their old pack, to the day the hunters burned it all down, Zahra let it all pour out of her.

She imagined others might find the act cathartic in some way, but to Zahra, this was a terrifying re-creation of the horror through which she'd lived, and carried around with her every day of her life.

The second Zahra realized the alpha triad had figured out what she'd done, to the day she was found guarding her parents' graves, the memories rushed out as if waiting for this moment at freedom. Days so dark, Zahra had willingly blocked them out, followed by years of isolation and loneliness, overtook her. Before she even realized what was happening, Zahra found herself in her friend's arms, both crying at a past neither of them could escape.

"I'm so sorry, Zahra."

"This is why I didn't want you to know. None of this is your fault. It never was. Evil things happen to good and bad people alike. From what we know, we are probably facing an evil that will be spreading. There won't be any time to worry about the past when we're fighting to ensure we have a future."

Rose's eyes seemed to glow gold around her irises. Not in the *I'm about to tear you apart* way, but more of a warm, comforting feeling. "How is it that you're the one consoling me when it was you who suffered horribly?"

"I've had a lot more time with these memories than you have. Everything dulls over time, even this."

Rose straightened her back and dried her tears. "Jewel will take a look at your injuries and formulate a plan to help repair what's been done to you."

Zahra held no illusions when it came to her throat being healed, and her voice returned to her. However, it wasn't hard to recognize that Rose needed some hope to hold on to.

"We'll see what happens, but you've got to understand I've made my peace with this. I accept that I will never be able to speak aloud again. Maybe this is penance for forcing my will on someone else, or perhaps the gods gave me the gift for that one purpose. After all, you are the reincarnation of a goddess critical to fighting back the collector demons. Either way, what's done is done." Zahra didn't want anyone getting their hopes up when it might well be an impossible situation.

"Allow me to at least try," Rose implored. "As you pointed out, I have the powers of a goddess, and Raz is even stronger. Between the two of us, there has to be a way to return what's been stolen from you."

Zahra couldn't help but smile at her friend's determination to fix what had been done. *"If it will make you feel any better about this, then you're welcome to try."*

"Thank you." The sounds of people pacing coming from the hallway outside Zahra's door were a pretty good indication their mates were close to the edge of their patience. "Should we let them in?"

"We should, before one of them turns furry and goes through the door," Zahra joked, trying to dispel the heaviness in the room. She was emotionally and physically exhausted. All she wanted to do now was rest in John's arms while she tried to push all those memories back into the box where they belonged.

The door opened almost immediately, and Zahra found herself in her big bear's arms. *Perfect.*

"We will arrange everything," Rose announced before Mason carried her out of Zahra's bedroom. "We will figure out a way to fix this."

Once the doors closed, Zahra sank further into John's arms. All the while, knowing there was no fix for her no matter how much anyone wished it.

"Will you stay here with me?" Zahra asked her mate.

"There is no other place in this universe I'd rather be, my love."

Chapter Four

As delicately as possible, Raz turned the pages of an ancient tome brought to her by a band of Caracal shifters from Northern Egypt. The shifter world had begun closing ranks as the number of collector demon sightings rose as they started showing up in several spots across the globe.

The last time those vile creatures passed through the veil, they wiped out an entire barrio outside Barcelona, Spain. That had been four days ago. There was no doubt in Raz's mind that the demons were growing stronger at a much faster rate as incidents of possessions in human hosts and widespread attacks increased in severity.

Shifters were uniting for the more significant battles ahead. As for humans, they blamed the dramatic uptick in violence on everything from video games and the Internet to environmental stressors and the phases of the moon's rotation or some other nonsense. When humans finally learned the truth, Raz imagined it would be like telling them that the boogeyman really does exist.

When that day came, humans would be forced to concede their spot on the top of the food chain, if it was ever theirs to begin with. In the human world, they were used to fighting foes they could touch and kill, restricted by the limitations their reality presented. The old ways were lost on them and banished to myth. When in truth, those myths, fables, and folklore would be the only thing standing between them and destruction.

Raz ran the palm of her hand over her swollen belly as her baby stretched out, or at least that's what it felt like. Weeks away from her due date, and she still hadn't been able to connect with the baby growing inside of her. Even with Doc's repeated reassurances that all was well, Raz couldn't help but worry. She could sense every last shifter in her pack, except for her own child.

She'd refused to be told her baby's gender after the fetal anatomy scan was completed about halfway through her pregnancy. Axel and Zander had sworn Doc to secrecy to make sure no one found out before the birth, though she doubted Doc would have uttered a word about it.

Still, Raz was left feeling lacking in some way due to the strength of the block in place. Did her child not wish to connect with her? Was some type of force keeping her baby from communicating? Was her baby sick or suffering?

Raz shook her head to clear these troubling thoughts. It would do her and her baby no good to become overwhelmed by what-ifs.

Returning her attention to the pages in front of her, which were initially written on papyrus, and in ancient hieratic, Raz didn't have the first clue why she suddenly understood the history and incantations the book outlined. The only logical answer had to be that her new ability was another power gifted to her by the Warrior Goddess Avra to aid them in the war to come.

A particular page in the second half of the book kept calling her back until Raz finally gave in and read the passage with more in-depth thought. Though the title, "Protectors of the Light," didn't seem to have the information they required in this particular situation. The text spoke of the ones who possessed something described as the Light of Heka.

The text was vague at best, diluted by time, but it spoke of the one who held a light of power, in the same respect as Ra, the sun god. Though little was known about these people and barely a page was written, Raz could feel her entire body humming at attention with every cell on alert. For some reason, these Protectors of the Light were essential, not only to shifters as a whole but to Raz personally.

The urgency sank in, making Raz unsettled and fearful, two emotions she'd hoped she'd left behind inside the hunters' cages. Seconds later and without warning, an excruciating pain tore through her belly, ripping a pain-filled scream from her throat. Axel and Xander were by her side moments later, in time to witness a gush of fluid cover the chair Raz was sitting on.

Before she could even register what was happening, Axel scooped her up into his arms and was carrying her down the hallway leading out of the triad's private rooms and into the main areas of the pack house.

The rooms around her flew by in a blur until moments later, Doc's calm face came into view accompanied by the bright lights over the top of the surgical table in the pack's medical clinic.

Raz felt the confusion of her pack through the link but had no time to assure everyone as her pain continued to worsen. Shifters, by nature, could handle a great deal of pain. This, however, was on an entirely new level.

"Well, Matriarch, it seems to be time for your baby to be born," Doc Hanley announced cheerfully.

"No, it's too soon," Raz cried. Her baby wasn't ready. She had weeks of her pregnancy remaining. "It's not safe."

"The baby will not wait," Doc explained while covering her with blankets, and his assistant, Caine, began pulling out various instruments.

"Everything will be okay, my love," Xander assured while Axel watched every move Doc and Caine made with an unblinking stare.

Her two mates handled situations differently. Axel had to retain control over conditions, and Xander allowed his emotions to lead. This didn't mean either of them loved her any more than the other; it was merely the way they were, and she loved them equally.

The muscles around her abdomen squeezed her tight and took her breath away. Raz knew with every fiber of her being that this protector of the light possessed the Light of Heka, and they needed to find this protector now.

"We need to find a being referred to as the protector of the light. Whoever it is possesses the shielding light of Heka," Raz gritted out between clenched teeth.

"Where do we find one?" Axel asked, believing her without question, not once taking his gaze off what Doc was doing. The confident mole shifter, with glasses as thick as her baby finger and a heart of gold, didn't even flinch at the intensity Axel was displaying.

"I don't know, the gods didn't see fit to tell me, though I'm certain we need one to make sure our baby survives," Raz went on to explain between moans of pain.

"There's no time to be looking for anyone," Doc Hanley advised. "Your baby is coming, we can't wait, Matriarch."

"Pray to the Gods that one finds us in time, or I'm certain all this is going to turn out badly." Raz knew they were out of time. Why wouldn't the Gods have shown her the passage in the old text sooner so that they could have searched for whoever these creatures might be?

Marian, her mother-in-law, and Nanna, a gifted Mage like Raz, peeked in following a quick knock on the door. Their pale faces were their first sign that things had gone from bad to worse. Nanna gave voice to the second sign.

"We're under attack."

***

"We have to move," John commanded his warriors as they gathered in the large yard behind the clan house. "Our allies are under attack by a horde of collector demons and need our help."

Zahra stood watching from the back patio as clan members gathered so Rose could teleport them over to the neighboring wolf pack. Apparently, their matriarch was in labor when the demons chose to attack.

Zahra had thought that wasn't a coincidence. Raz was the reincarnation of a strong goddess, and the only chance of the demons getting the upper hand on her and her mates would be by attacking while the matriarch was giving birth, and her mates were busy protecting them.

Although Zahra had managed to shift back into her wolf form since telling Rose the truth about their joined past, Jewel had told Zahra her voice had been irreparably harmed, as she'd suspected.

Rose hadn't given up on finding a fix, no matter how many times Zahra had told her that she was happy this way. She imagined it would take more time for her friend to come to grips with the truth that Zahra would never be able to speak aloud again. John had moved into her suite since the day she'd told Rose the truth.

In a rush of motion, Rose, Mason, and Riker came running out of the clan house, and Zahra padded over to join John at his side. Zahra had never seen a wolf Rose's size before. She towered over the bears.

Zahra would fight by her mate's side to protect Raz and her baby. Zahra would have done so no matter what, but some unknown force inside her made it feel imperative she joined the fight.

"Remember to remove the demons from their hosts, you must kill the host." At the look of shock on a few clan members' faces, John continued. "As of the last attack in Barcelona, we have determined that unlike millennia ago, we can't force them out of their hosts without killing the host. The matriarch can remove the demon with a touch of her hand, but only one teenaged male has ever survived.

"Until we can figure out a way to save the hosts, you must battle them to the death. Do not allow your sympathy to cloud your judgment, or the demon will take your life along with its host without a second thought. Collector demons thrive and gain strength by the number of souls they gather. Matriarch Rose will trap as many as she can before the demons have a chance to take the souls back across the veil."

Brutal but true. Zahra had been learning from John more about the warrior goddesses and the veil between their two worlds. That veil had been thinning over thousands of years due to the amount of evil and corruption in this world, and that called to the collector demons, making their transitions more and more frequent.

"I'm coming with you," Zahra announced as the alpha triad joined the warriors and clan members preparing for battle. Various weapons and armor were distributed to those fighting in their human forms, while the others shifted into their bears. Hawks from the cast that took refuge on Porda land had already shifted and were perched on the backs of several bears.

John's response was immediate and crushing. "No."

"That wasn't a question."

John lowered down onto one knee so that they were on the same level since Zahra was in her wolf form. "You are not trained as a warrior, my mate. I will not risk losing you."

"You're not risking anything. This is my choice. Besides, Marie is going and she hasn't been trained. I'm no different than her." Though she doubted John would see it that way.

"There's a big difference. Marie is an over eight-hundred-pound bear when she shifts," John said.

He might as well have slapped her across the face. *"I see, and I'm merely a minor wolf?"*

John looked ready to say something more when Riker abruptly cut him off. "If Zahra wishes to fight by our sides, we welcome her. She is a member of this clan."

Zahra felt the warmth of acceptance. She was indeed part of the clan.

"Let's go," Mason ordered, and everyone joined hands. Riker placed his hand on John's shoulder, and with a look of resignation and fear, John reached for Zahra.

She and John would be having a long talk when this was over. Zahra had been taking care of herself for a long time and didn't need a mate telling her what to do. She knew a war coming, and they'd need all the help they could get to defeat the enemy.

The moment his hand touched her fur, the world swirled around her. Rose had been gifted with the power of teleportation, and by linking together, they could all share the gift and travel at once.

One moment Zahra was looking into her mate's concerned gaze, and the next, she was in an unfamiliar forest alongside other shifters fighting off what appeared to be humans in different stages of decomposition.

Some had rotting flesh hanging from their protruding bones while others were missing parts of their hosts' bodies, either an arm, hand, or leg. It reminded Zahra of one of her mother's old books that she'd called a horror story. Unfortunately, this horror story had come to life.

John had explained to her that when a demon took a host, there had to be an initial evil living within that host. The higher the level of darkness, the faster they decomposed. By the looks of what remained of some of these people, there were some seriously demented assholes out in the world among the innocent.

Their group scattered in all directions, mowing down demons as they went. However, before John released her, he said, "Be safe, my love. You are everything to this old bear."

"I love you, as well. There had better not be a scratch on you when we celebrate our victory. You don't want to see me angry." If John got hurt, she'd go full-on psycho-wolf.

Before more could be said, a short man with a scraggly gray beard attacked them. John easily dodged the swipe of the demon's blade while Zahra tore at the guy's arm with her sharp claws until he released his weapon. John spun around behind the man with such speed that the host didn't have a chance to stop her mate from relieving him of his head. A black misty shadow rose out of the host body, but before it had an opportunity to make its getaway, Rose pulled it out of the air. As she gathered each demon before they had a chance to steal away with the soul and infect anyone else, their screams of rage filled the area. The power was another welcomed gift from the Goddess Thorne.

John shifted into his massive bear and began slicing through attackers with his sharp six-inch claws. Zahra sprinted toward the pack house, trying to head off a group of demons racing that way. Dodging a few bullets as she ran, she met up with another wolf she assumed was from this home pack, and they converged on the closest few demons nearing the house.

Together, along with a few bears, they defended the house with sharp teeth and claws until more shifters could arrive. A pair of tigers joined in the fight, surprising Zahra. She'd never seen tiger shifters before even though she knew Raz was a tigress.

Her old pack refused to interact with other shifters, and definitely not someone from a different species. Zahra loved that she was now able to be part of this world together with all the other species.

Once they had the last of this group of demons on the ground in pieces, Zahra took stock of what was happening around her. The pack house was on lockdown. Metal covers had been rolled down over every window, and she was positive that the thick wooden doors were barred from the inside. Their job was to keep these evil creatures from reaching the interior of the house, where many had sought shelter.

Zahra raked her claws across the throat of another host who had charged her, but the woman kept on coming. Considering they were essentially dead after the demons took them as hosts, bleeding to death was not a viable way of stopping them.

The idea was to inflict enough damage to make the demon leave the body. It was a gruesome thing to have to do, but at this point, the shifters had no other choice. These creatures would carry on killing everyone in their paths, shifter and human alike. They were unstoppable until they fully decomposed and fell apart or were diced into pieces, causing their bodies to turn into dust.

Her throat slash didn't even slow the female demon down, leaving Zahra open to attack on her unprotected side. The burn of the blade as it scraped against her ribs confirmed her mistake. There was no time to assess the damage as more collector demons stumbled out from the tree line. Their jerky movements increased with their state of decomposition, giving them a creepy, staggering gate.

Before her attacker had a chance to take another swipe at her with the blade, Zahra tore off its hand. A roar alerted her to Marie as the colossal bear mowed down three demons with a swipe of her massive paw and claws, including the one Zahra was going head to head with. She had to admit that a bear shifter was like a force of nature.

"Thank you, Marie."

"You're welcome. Call me if you need me," Marie said through their clan link. She had liked Marie since first meeting her at the ruins of Zahra's old pack. The young woman had been through her own personal hell but welcomed Zahra with open arms.

The two separated, and Zahra headed for the other side of the main house where most of the battle was raging. The wall of glass doors leading from the large patio and into the house was barricaded with hastily erected timbers. Broken glass could be seen through the gaps, but as of yet, the interior hadn't been breached.

Various species of shifters stood shoulder-to-shoulder fighting to protect their matriarch and her baby, as well as the other shifters inside the house. This was the type of shifter society Zahra wanted to belong to, not to be hidden away.

She jumped onto the back of the nearest demon and sank her long canines into the back of its neck. The creature struggled to knock Zahra off, but she held on while digging her claws into its spine until she reached the bone and severed it. The demon collapsed, and seconds later turned to dust.

The injury to Zahra's ribs pulsed with pain, and she could scent her own blood. Looking around, she could see demons still stepping out of the forest. Zahra had no idea where so many were coming from. It wasn't as if the North Woods Pack was near any major cities or human towns.

Several of her fellow shifters were injured but continued to fight, but far too many lay motionless on the ground. John was nowhere to be seen, and neither were Rose and her mates. Thankfully, Zahra could still sense her mate through their link, so she had to set her worry aside and keep fighting while hoping they were still fighting, as well.

A group of demons charged toward Zahra, and she barely had the chance to dodge out of their way. Gunshots began ringing out around her, and numerous shifters fell to the ground. The demons' host bodies were now throwing themselves at the barricaded wall of glass doors.

The glass shattered on the other side from the force of the blows. Somewhere in that building, a baby was being born, while death surrounded them. This was not the way things should be. A child's birth shouldn't be marred by death. Zahra's anger and sadness drove her forward.

Without breaking stride, Zahra launched herself at the closest demon and then the next. It was a never-ending river of hosts, and these demons didn't seem to be in short supply. The cut to her ribs wasn't the last of her injuries, and she could feel herself weakening. One bullet caught Zahra in the right hind leg, knocking her to the ground in the middle of the fighting.

Demons turned on her immediately. Their bloody skeletal hands reached for her, but in the work of a moment the bloodthirsty assholes were sent flying several feet away. Zahra looked up in time to see John, laying waste to all those in front of him. She'd never seen such a skilled warrior who had every right to be a general. However, as more host bodies poured forward, John was quickly being overrun.

Zahra stood on three legs, dragging the fourth, and tried to make it to John's side. If she were to die, Zahra would do so fighting at her mate's side. The more she struggled, the angrier she became until something snapped deep inside her when her big bear was taken to the ground.

Words echoed through her head in a language Zahra had never heard before but somehow understood. Zahra listened to the first high-pitched cries of a newborn shifter before her body heated and lifted off the ground. The shock on John's face must have mirrored her own and those around her.

Anger like nothing she'd ever felt before ran through her body at the carnage left below by the collector demons bent on killing that baby. Her neck and throat burned more than the first times it had been cut, and Zahra would have screamed if she could have. The fighting raged on below, but the only sound she could hear was the distressed cries of a baby.

Zahra understood her body was no longer her own. Bullets ricocheted off an invisible barrier around her so that not one of them struck her body. She fought to be freed even though there was no way she'd stay above it all safe while others died below. Zahra didn't pretend to understand what was happening, but she'd be damned if she sat by and allowed it.

A knife-edge of pain pierced Zahra's chest and through her heart, making her body convulse violently before everything around her went dark.

John's voice crying out was the last thing she heard. *"Zahra."*

Chapter Five

John fought with everything he had to get to his mate but was repeatedly forced back by the horde of demons surrounding her. He knew to his core that the tide had turned, and it wouldn't be long before the pack house was overrun. No matter how hard and long each shifter fought, they were still severely outnumbered.

He watched helplessly as Zahra was lifted into the air above them. A bright yellow glow radiated from her body, and she'd shifted back into her human form. The sight of her many wounds sent him into a rage that he gladly used against the demons near him.

John had no idea if it was good or evil at play here, but he wanted his mate back on the ground. However, he thought better of it considering the multitude of hosts the collector demons had been able to infect that now swarmed the house.

The ground shook violently, throwing the creatures off balance. Zahra's light engulfed the pack house and surrounding area. Her usually blue eyes opened wide, containing the same golden light, and Zahra gazed down.

"Stop." Her voice boomed over the battlefield, and even though John was sure that his mate's lips hadn't moved, she had, in fact, spoken aloud and not through the link. In the next instant, every last host body froze where they stood. The collector demons who'd taken possession of these human hosts appeared to be struggling to make their bodies move.

John stepped away from the five he'd been fighting and took a long look around. The other shifters who were able stood, and they too tried to take stock of what was happening. It was eerily quiet, except for the low growls coming from the angry collector demons as they fought against whatever Zahra had done to them. Rose, Mason, and Riker came running around the corner of the house, sliding to a stop at seeing a golden Zahra floating above them all.

"Your evil does not belong here," Zahra spoke again without moving her lips. This time, John was confident the words were spoken aloud. *"Leave."*

That one word vibrated through everyone and everything in the area, and almost immediately, the host bodies began turning to dust where they stood. Before the demons had a chance of escaping, Rose raised her hands to the sky and gathered the shadowy assholes with her powers gifted to her by the Goddess Thorne.

Their rage-filled shouts and cries filled the air moments before Rose destroyed them, making it impossible for those particular demons to infect anyone else.

With the demons and their hosts gone, Zahra began to lower toward the ground, still glowing brightly. Her body appeared to be healed and covered in a flowing golden gown emblazoned with symbols from the Eye of Ra and an ankh, the symbol of life.

Once her feet touched the ground, Zahra's golden gaze turned to John, who had shifted back into his human form. *"We are not finished, my love."* She held out her glowing hand to him, and he took it.

"Are you in there, Zahra?" John had to ask. He wanted to know if his mate was back in control.

"I am, my big bear." Zahra's loving smile further confirmed she was healthy and safe.

Shifters hurried to aid the injured and fallen as Zahra led him to the back doors of the pack house, followed by Rose, Mason, and Riker. With a touch of her free hand to the wooden barricades, they vanished, leaving the way open for them to enter the pack house.

John could feel the calming and healing energies being spread by Matriarch Rose as they passed through a room full of frightened women and children. A team of enforcers stood among them: the last line of protection should the pack house have been breached.

Zahra continued farther into the house, passing room after room, until they came to a hallway teeming with enforcers. The sadness and grief were palpable, slamming into their small group like a brick wall. Something was wrong.

Not one of the men tried to stop Zahra from walking past them and toward what John knew to be the infirmary. He could hear the occasional sobbing coming from the room, and his heart fell. This would be where Matriarch Raz would have been giving birth to her baby.

Without stopping, Zahra opened the door and led them into a scene John prayed he'd never be forced to see again. The alpha triad was on the far end of the room. Raz was lying on a bed and being held by her mates, Axel, and Xander. Her sobs were heartbreaking.

A few feet away, Doc Hanley and Caine stood hunched over a smaller table ablaze in light. By the amount of blood present, John suspected the baby had been born but didn't make it. *Shit.*

Rose rushed forward and took up a position at Doc's side, while Mason and Riker closed the door behind them and stood guard. No one would be disturbing the grief-stricken triad as Rose, Doc, and Caine worked feverishly to get the small baby to react and breathe.

Doc called for instruments and ordered more suction as he attempted to intubate the pale baby. John got a glimpse of the baby's tiny head, covered in dark orange and blonde hair like Raz's. Rose used everything at her disposal to help, but not one of her powers would change the dawning truth. The baby hadn't survived.

The Doc's and Alpha Axel's eyes met from across the room. The alpha wolf's pain was confirmation of John's assessment of the situation. All movement around the table stopped, and Rose returned to Mason's and Riker's waiting arms. His heart was crushed for his friends and the tiny life that wouldn't have a chance to grow and bloom.

Zahra released John's hand and took Doc's place at the side of the bed. Her body began to glow even brighter, finally garnering Raz's attention.

"The Protector of the Light," Raz rasped out between sobs. Her eyes getting impossibly big, she said, "Zahra is the bearer of the Eye of Ra...the Light and Shield of Heka. I beg you, save my baby."

John wasn't sure what the matriarch meant by what she claimed his mate to be, but by the shocked reaction of her mates, it had to be something of great importance.

Zahra didn't respond but remained entirely focused on the small form lying in what John realized was an open incubator. She placed her golden hand over the top of the pale baby, and Zahra's eyes filled with tears. John wrapped Zahra in his arms to comfort her, and as he did, he hoped he could help in some small way.

The glow deepened and encompassed his body the moment they touched, unlike earlier when John had held her hand. Zahra's body began to tremble. John braced her against his chest while the glow covered the baby as well.

The room fell silent. No one dared to speak, everyone watching Zahra to see if somehow she could perform a miracle.

John had no idea what was happening to his mate and only prayed none of this hurt her in any way. Soon the glow became so bright that John had no other choice but to close his eyes, along with everyone else in the room.

"Awake." Zahra's voice rang out.

By the shouts coming from other parts of the pack house, the glow must have gone even farther then he'd thought. He wasn't entirely sure how long they stood there, but when the light began to fade, John looked back up to find that his mate was now holding the baby though he hadn't felt her move. The triad's baby was now bundled in a thick blanket, with skin that was now pink, and her little chest was rising and falling with the breath of life.

Zahra's body returned to her usual un-glowing self before she crossed the distance to stand before Raz. *"She wishes to be in her mother's arms."*

Both Axel and Xander fell to their knees in front of Zahra. "Blessed be the Eye of Ra for saving our daughter's life, we offer ours to you for this irreplaceable gift," Axel announced for them both, shocking John even further.

Zahra brushed her fingertips over the baby girl's cheek and smiled wide before answering. *"You owe me nothing. Your lives are going to be far too busy keeping up with this little angel to be concerned over any sort of debt to me. She's a fighter and is going to be a handful, like her mother, I'm told."* Zahra placed the now fussing baby into Raz's arms, and she quieted immediately, and the triad welcomed their daughter, surrounding her in love.

John's happiness evaporated, replaced immediately by a sense of something being terribly wrong moments before Zahra walked into his arms and collapsed. Quickly, he lifted his mate and placed her on an empty nearby bed. Doc Hanley began examining her while John begged any and all gods that were listening. They must protect this brave woman whom he loved beyond comprehension, and could never go on without her by his side.

***

The nauseating scent of burning fur seemed so familiar to her now that Zahra didn't even bother jumping up. She knew far too well if she bothered to look she'd find herself lying back beside her parents' graves in her old pack's territory. The nightmare would play out as it always did. Her village would burst into flames while hunters killed everyone in sight. Everyone except her.

There was no need for Zahra to even open her eyelids and watch the slaughter taking place around her to know that it was happening. She couldn't help but wonder if a day would ever come when the nightmares would stop, while at the same time accepting that they wouldn't.

"Don't be so sure of that," a feminine voice said from somewhere behind her.

Zahra leapt to her feet so fast that she almost lost her footing when she realized she wasn't in her wolf form as she'd always been during these nightmares. Instead, Zahra was fully dressed in jeans and a short-sleeved shirt, standing by what appeared to be rows of gigantic carved stone pillars.

Hot sand shifted between her bare toes even though she was in the shade of these giants covered in pristine hieroglyphics. Zahra's knowledge of Egypt was limited to a single picture book her mom had saved for her from her mother's childhood. It was disconcerting knowing more about the past than the here and now.

She spun in a circle but found she was alone. The sun was high in the sky, and for as far as she could see, there was only sand.

"Where the hell am I?"

"Karnak. In ancient Thebes, before the humans lost their way."

Zahra turned to her left and found an older woman standing only a few feet away from her and leaning against an obelisk as if she didn't have a care in the world. Zahra was positive the stranger hadn't been there moments ago. She would have noticed someone dressed in a deep purple robe trimmed in gold.

"Who are you?"

"Dear, you don't have to speak through your mind any longer," she said. "At least not here."

Zahra reached for her neck, and for the first time in over half a century, she didn't feel the uneven and torn flesh of her scars. Her skin was smooth and unmarred by any damage.

"What," Zahra began but remembered what the woman said. "W-what's going on? Where is John?"

"Millennia, in the future, I'm afraid."

"Who are you?" The feel and sound of actual words coming from her lips was intoxicating. "How did you fix me?"

The older woman smiled at Zahra indulgently as if speaking to a child, but for some reason, the behavior didn't annoy her. "My name is Hathor, and in this realm, all physical injuries and abnormalities are healed. However, when you return to your own, the cuts will as well."

"This realm?" That didn't sound good. "Did I die?"

Zahra remembered blacking out for a minute before waking back up and kicking some serious demon butt. The baby…Raz's baby was brought back to life. Did she dream all that? Had she died when she passed out and never woke up again? John. What about her mate?

"I see your mind is racing, let me assure you, you are alive and so is your mate."

"So, that means the baby is alive as well."

"And the demons turned back to dust," Hathor explained, waving her slender hands around in the air. "All is as it should be."

Zahra took a deep breath and let it out slowly. "Okay, then why am I here with you and not with my mate?"

"I needed to have a word with you," Hathor said, acting like standing here in the middle of Karnak was a regular thing. "Don't worry, your unconscious body is back among your people."

Zahra was not having the best of days, and was feeling disoriented in the extreme. Fighting demons, being stabbed and shot, having her body taken over, and bringing a baby back to life were only a few things she still had to deal with. She didn't want to play any games or be talked in circles.

"What do you want from me?" She enunciated every word to make sure Hathor understood she'd been pushed far enough. Goddess or not, someone had some serious explaining to do. Control of her life had been taken away long ago. Now that Zahra had John and a home again, she would be damned if she'd allow it to be taken away so quickly.

A spark of light passed through Hathor's dark eyes. "You do not fear me, a Goddess, an Eye of Ra?"

"Of course I do, I'm not an idiot." Zahra wasn't so far gone that she didn't realize the danger. "But you happened to have caught me on a particularly shitty day."

The sides of Hathor's lips ticked up slightly. "Walk with me."

Hathor turned and walked deeper into the temple. Zahra imagined now wouldn't be a good time to mention that she had no idea who Hathor was, or the eye of Ra. With no other choice, Zahra followed the goddess past rows of carved stone figures. She was getting more and more freaked out, as the gaze from each statue seemed to follow her.

"Don't concern yourself with them, they've always been nosy. Gossips, each of them."

That didn't help calm Zahra one bit. They continued on, passing stunning walls of hieroglyphs, one after another. The pictures in her mom's book showed them broken and without color, but to Zahra, what appeared before her seemed brand new.

"Yes, your mother's pictures are correct. What you see here is the majesty before the fall of the Egyptian Empire, and the beginning of humanity's attempt at...progress." The way in which Hathor growled the last word gave Zahra a pretty good indication of what the goddess thought of their progress.

"Great, so you're inside my head, reading my thoughts." Zahra shouldn't have been shocked.

Before Hathor could answer, a tall man wearing a white tunic with a thick leather belt came to join them. He was the only person Zahra had seen so far other than Hathor.

"The remaining legions have been driven back, Goddess Hathor, and the veil is holding them for now," he said before turning to face Zahra. "Well done, Goddess Zahra."

"Goddess?" Zahra's throat went dry.

"Thank you, Thoth," Hathor answered. "We will talk soon."

Thoth nodded and walked away.

When Hathor turned to continue down the corridor, Zahra's patience had come to an end. No more waiting. "I'm not taking another step until you start talking. What did he mean when he called me a goddess?"

Hathor looked at her oddly and said, "Very well," before snapping her fingers.

You would think Zahra should have been used to being whisked to other locations by now, but nope. Though it was suddenly dark, the familiar churning in her stomach confirmed that she was indeed airborne and traveling. To where, she had no idea. Maybe she should have thought a bit longer before issuing an order to Hathor.

When she felt solid ground back beneath her bare feet, Zahra didn't even bother waiting for her vision to clear. She ran several feet away from Hathor and said, "Stop doing that. I'm going to throw up all over the next person that tries it."

The chorus of laughter got her attention, and Zahra swung around to face a small group of women. Four women sat on various pieces of carved wooden furniture covered in symbols while two other seats remained empty. A tiled pool of water sat behind them, and a large disc circled by snakes hung from the wall above it. There were other symbols, but Zahra had no idea what they represented. John would know. She wanted her mate back.

"You'll be seeing him soon enough, young one," the woman wearing a red dress and a large golden lion pendant around her neck assured. "My name is Sekhmet and welcome. Please take a seat. We have much to discuss."

The goddess held out her hand in the direction of a large chair covered in thick cushions with various images of wolves carved into its dark wood. Hathor sat in the other empty seat adorned with large cow horns. For the first time, she noticed Hathor had a similar necklace, but her pendant depicted a cow.

It appeared that each woman wore a golden pendant, each with different designs matching their own chairs.

"I am Bastet," the woman with an intricate cat pendant said. "This is Wadjet," she continued while pointing toward a woman wearing a cobra pendant.

"And I am Mut," said the last of the group of five. Her chair had an impressive set of wings, and she wore a bright blue strange crown.

"Okay, okay, now that we have introductions out of the way. Tell me, Zahra, what makes you so damn special?" the one named Sekhmet asked. Zahra was positive that the eyes on her lioness pendant glowed red.

That's my question.

Chapter Six

John stood, watching over his mate. Zahra hadn't woken since she'd collapsed into his arms over five days ago. They were back on Porda Clan land, and John had her safely tucked away in one of the bedrooms beneath the clan house that he'd claimed as theirs.

The tunnels and rooms, built well below the ground in case of attack, didn't resemble dirt passages or chiseled-out walls in some dark pit resembling those of hibernating wild bears, although, as bear shifters, being miles underground did hold an appeal.

This underground city had taken over two hundred years to build and had been undertaken after Mason and Ricker's mother, the former matriarch, had received a troubling premonition of danger to come. Their neighboring friends had followed the bears' lead and built their own versions of the same. Though only the Porda Clan and North Woods Pack were connected.

In truth, the entire complex covered acres of land and resembled more of a high-end hotel and complex than anything else. Over eighty percent of the clan had done the same as him, while the remainder were busy boarding up the houses left empty. All supplies and clan house staff had already been moved down, and another group handled the shutdown of the brewery.

After the initial battle on the North Woods Pack lands, the demons had remained quiet for days. Unfortunately, in the last twenty-four hours, the bastards had made up for it. Reports were coming in from across the globe about humans turning on each other in the streets.

Social media channels were flooded with pictures and videos of injured and decomposing human hosts chasing people through stores and down streets. Bodies of the uninfected were left where they fell, while hosts left piles of dust and ashes. The soulless black eyes of these hosts seemed even more significant than before, more menacing somehow.

Leaders of countries were announcing a state of emergency, along with the President of the United States. Their first response was to send in the military. Which was all fine and good until that trained personnel turned into hosts and started attacking the same people they were supposed to be protecting.

The outside world was quickly turning into a war zone, and the sooner they had all their people safely below ground, the better.

John rolled onto his side and wrapped his scarred arm around a still-unconscious Zahra. Doc had been making regular visits while setting up the infirmary on the lower communal levels. According to Jewel, Zahra was physically healthy and would wake when she was ready.

New additions had appeared on his mate's body on the backs and palms of her hands. In black, like tattoos, were the symbols depicting the Eye of Ra. Raz had called Zahra the protector of the light, the Eye of Ra, and the shield of Heka. However, until she woke, John didn't know what that meant, and if Zahra understood her new powers. Above all, Zahra was his mate, and the woman he loved, with whom he wanted to build a life, even though, given the state of the world, John didn't know how long that life would be. Whatever time they had, he wanted it with her.

A soft knock sounded, and John kissed Zahra's cheek before getting up, grabbing his shirt, and putting it on while walking to the door. Marie stood a couple feet away from the entryway. She was accompanied by Freckles, Rose's orange and white cat, and Marie carried the same book she had the last three times she'd come to sit with Zahra while John continued his duties as Porda's general. Especially now that the rest of the world was going to hell, John had to ensure the safety of his people.

"Hello, Marie. What chapter are the two of you on now?" John asked. He'd walked in on Marie reading aloud to Zahra a few times when returning from his duties.

"Six," she answered. "Jerome is about to propose to Adele, but her ex is trying to stop him."

"Romance, good choice," John said. "We could all use a happily-ever-after right about now."

"Agreed. Any improvement?"

"No change, I'm afraid."

"She'll wake up soon, I feel it."

"I hope you're right," John said and stepped out into the hallway as Marie entered. "I shouldn't be any later than four. If Zahra wakes up while I'm gone—"

"I know, call you immediately and reassure her that you are close and haven't abandoned her. But honestly, Zahra will understand, especially with what's happening out there."

"True enough. I feel guilty about having to leave her. That's what's bothering me. Either way, I won't be too long."

Marie nodded and continued on into the bedroom while John shut the main door behind him. It still felt odd at times having Marie, the bear who'd challenged the matriarch, as a trusted member of the clan. However, after it was discovered what her parents had done to manipulate the poor woman, what had happened began to make sense.

John took one of the four main stairwells up to the surface. There were several more minor stairwells in case of emergency, but everyone typically traveled using these. Another useful attribute of shifter life was their strength and speed. For the most part, elevators weren't needed. Though they did have a service elevator for getting the large pieces of furniture down.

When John reached the top, he didn't come out of a conventional doorway. What was the use of having hidden underground bunkers if you made the entrance easy to find? Instead, John surfaced inside a larger cave that, among other things, housed their hybrid land vehicles.

Several clan members were busy moving boxes of various sizes containing supplies deeper into the tunnel. Warriors stood at the ready, guarding all entrances. They'd set up sensors across their lands so that even when they were beneath the surface, they'd have firsthand knowledge of anything moving in the area.

He jumped into one of the trucks and took off toward the main house, driving through what used to be a thriving town of shifter-owned businesses now standing empty and dark. The vehicles on the road were all headed in the opposite direction toward the safety of the bunkers.

Rose was already moved into the bunkers helping calm clan shifters as well as various other groups of shifters who'd come to the Porda Clan for safety. Mason and Riker remained aboveground until every last shifter had moved into their new homes.

Larger shipping trucks were pulling out of the laneway leading to the main house when he arrived. The last remaining items were scheduled to be loaded by the end of the day, along with the final few clan members.

John parked behind the house and was caught off guard by what he saw. The hinges on the truck door groaned as he opened it to stand and stare out at the grim sight. Each of the beautiful community homes set behind the main clan house now stood boarded up in an attempt to protect them while away. The whole area felt shaded in gray.

He remembered all the lazy summer days playing in and around those houses as a young cub with his friends. John had been born and grew up here. Porda Clan lands were part of him, in his blood, and now his own children may never have a chance to experience the same joys and freedom ever again. John swore on his life that he'd fight to ensure further generations had the opportunity to safely play in the sun.

"Shocking, isn't it?" Mason said from behind him. John had scented him long before Mason made it this close. They'd all have to be on guard from now on to their surroundings.

"Depressing, gut-wrenching, any of those words will do." His mate's condition, along with this, made John melancholy and angry at the same time.

"I remember when you tried to kick my ass over by Donovan's house, for running through some sand fort you'd been building." Mason chuckled at the memory.

"I was three, and I would have done it too if my mom hadn't come out and stopped me."

"Keep telling yourself that, sand-boy," Mason ribbed.

John couldn't help but laugh, even as his heart broke.

Mason laid his hand on John's shoulder and gave it a squeeze. "No matter what happens, they can't take our memories."

John clenched his jaw and took strength from what the alpha had said. "No, the bastards can't take those, and our children will know this type of freedom again."

"Yes, they will, my friend."

***

"Special," Zahra replied. "I don't know what you mean."

Sekhmet didn't seem satisfied with her answer. "Special. Exceptional. Rare. Unique. I'm speaking your English language, am I not?"

"Down, down, big kitty," Mut admonished. "You always get testy when a new Eye is chosen. Remember, this doesn't mean you are less in any way."

Zahra had no idea what was going on, but since when had that ever stopped her before. "Excuse me, Eye?"

"Yes, you have been chosen as the Eye of Ra, same as us five," Wadjet answered while flicking her fingers above her head and toward the other four.

"I'm sorry, but I don't know what that means."

"Of course, you don't. You're that wild one living full time in your animal form," Sekhmet spat out.

Zahra's anger flared, and strangely her palms began to burn. "Yes, that's me. Would you like to truly see how wild I can be?" To make sure she wasn't misunderstood, she flashed a sharp canine in Sekhmet's direction.

Sekhmet's eyes flashed a golden hue, she raised her hand toward Zahra, and it began to glow. Zahra had milliseconds to respond with her own, now shining, hand. *What the hell?* Without thought or understanding, she pointed her palm at Sekhmet as a light shot from the lioness's hand at Zahra.

The same type of glow flowed from Zahra's own palm, slamming into the other beam of light and deflecting it harmlessly away. Sekhmet abruptly stood and tried again, only this time Zahra was ready and a bit quicker on the draw. Surprising herself, she managed to knock the goddess back onto her seat.

Then it hit her. She was trading blows with an actual goddess. Zahra pulled back and looked down at the symbols pulsing on her hands to find the same mark on the goddess's skin as well. "Can someone explain to me what is going on, instead of attacking me?"

Bastet, the cat goddess, stood and said, "Enough out of you, Sekhmet. Ra has chosen us a new sister, and you will not defy him."

The ground shook, and the sky rumbled, appearing to be in agreement with Bastet.

Zahra looked around at the five of them, still bewildered by everything, but having apparently already gained an enemy. "I honestly have no idea why I'm here. I don't want to be here, let's make that clear, and I certainly do not want to take anything that isn't mine. Now, if one of you, well, anyone other than the lioness over there, wants to ship me back to where I came from, I'd be thankful."

"You would reject the Sun God's choice?" Sekhmet asked, seeming shocked.

"First off, the choice for what?"

"You have been chosen to become the Eye of Ra. We defend the Sun God's rule against those who wish to bring disorder into his world. The collector demons are creating chaos with their actions and must be dealt with," Bastet explained as if this were public knowledge.

Zahra sank back down into her chair and began tracing the image of a bear, which had been carved into the wood, with the tips of her fingers. Upon closer inspection, she soon realized that there were bears interspersed among the wolf carvings on her seat.

"Tell me, will these powers be strong enough to help win the war?"

"Yes. In the same manner they've helped us defend against those that threatened with chaos since the beginning of time," Wadjet answered. Zahra caught a glimpse of her sharp cobra fangs.

"What's the catch?" Zahra asked. In her life, there'd always been one.

"Should you agree," Hathor's voice had taken on a deeper tone, "if you and your people fail to eradicate the collector demons before they kill all human life on the earth, your life becomes forfeit."

"How do we stop them from being infected? That's impossible."

"It would seem that way, but as you've noticed, shifters are inherently immune to infection. It's the humans who will be lost first. We cannot allow that to happen."

"Humans aren't our friends. They hunt us." These five had to know that.

"Yes, some of them do," Mut agreed. "But there are even more who do not."

"Because they don't know about us yet," Zahra stressed.

"That is untrue in cases, you will see," Mut defended.

"How can we save them from being infected? Sure, at the moment, it's only those with darkness in their souls becoming infected, but the collector demons are growing stronger. They will eventually overcome the remaining humans even if their souls aren't already dark."

By now, all six of them were again sitting in their seats aligned in a circle. Sekhmet didn't look happy, but she also didn't seem ready to decapitate Zahra, so she took that as a win for the moment.

"There are those humans who will not be infected. You need to find them and protect them," Bastet told her as if this were a simple task.

"And I'm supposed to know who these people are? Maybe run up to each human and hope I don't end up bringing an infected one into our midst to kill our children. That is if they don't try to kill me first." Okay, Zahra was getting pissy, but after everything, they were now supposed to forgive and forget the humans' actions. The wars, deaths, and destruction, brought in the name of human civilizations.

Zahra had done a great deal of reading since being brought to the Porda Clan. Her mate had an extensive library on both shifter and human histories and was shocked to find out that her pack wasn't even the worst offender when it came to cruelty in the world.

"I understand your misgivings about this," Bastet said, "however, those humans do have one thing in common. Each has shifter DNA inside of them." With that revelation the other shoe fell.

"How is that possible? I've never heard of such a thing." In all the books, there was no mention of these half-shifter humans.

"In most cases, the person has no idea they are part shifter. Some have increased natural abilities that are explained away as either excellence or being freakish. For example, the extended lives of people in certain parts of the Mediterranean are seen as results from a proper diet, red wine, or a way of life, and not the fact that several different shifter species like the Mediterranean weather.

"How about those Olympic athletes that run like a cheetah, or swim like a dolphin? On the reverse side of that coin, those with more unusual features, such as a tail which is removed at birth, or those humans who had exceptionally pronounced canine teeth having them filed down, and some with the ability to sense if someone is being truthful or lying being held as a witch. We had a hell of a time in Salem."

"To some, it's a blessing. While to others, it's a curse," Mut said.

"Why haven't we ever been told about them?" Zahra asked.

"Considering the tensions between humans and shifters, it was believed to be best to protect them from both sides," Hathor explained. "They are proof humans and shifters aren't that different."

Zahra had to admit Hathor had a point. Humans would have killed or captured them to study and experiment on, while shifters would have banished them as outcasts, unable to fully trust them.

"This isn't going to be easy."

"Doing the right thing never is," Sekhmet mumbled.

Zahra didn't even try to hide her growl. "Don't speak to me as if I hadn't witnessed my entire pack slaughtered by human hunters and relive it every time I close my eyes. Women and children gunned down for sport. There is a lot of bad blood between us." For a second, Sekhmet's expression lost a bit of its arrogance. "What happens if I refuse?"

"Then you will be returned to your life the same as you were before being chosen, at the exact moment you were chosen." Mut said the last few words slowly and with intention.

Zahra understood the ramifications. She'd be returned, powerless, to the point before she was lifted above the battle on North Woods Pack's territory. Moments before they would have been overrun by demon hosts while Raz was giving birth. Without the power of the Eye, Zahra wouldn't have been able to save the baby's life.

"And the lives of all those struck down in the battle itself," Hathor added.

"What?"

"When you brought Raz's daughter back to life, your passion for saving a life was extended out into the wolves' territory. Thus, healing all those injured or killed."

"You don't play fair, do you?" Zahra's choice had been already made, no matter her own distrust and anger at the humans. She would never reverse the good that had already been done. "I agree."

"Good," Mut announced. "We better get you back to your mate. He's been waiting long enough."

"Wait, how long have I been here?" A couple hours at most, she thought.

"Time travels differently between realities, but roughly ten of your days," Mut calculated.

"Ten days," Zahra yelled as the world shifted once again.

Bastet yelled back, "You'll learn how to control it all in time, same as you'll know who are those who need to be saved."

"Great. That's helpful," Zahra responded angrily.

Laughter was their reply.

Chapter Seven

Zahra's eyelids flew open, and she found herself in a darkened room. John's scent surrounded her, calming her immediately. She registered the weight of comfort his muscled arm across her waist provided. She held up her left hand to confirm that what she recalled hadn't been a dream, and sure enough, the Eye was on her hands in what appeared to be indelible ink. Next, she examined her throat. Ironically, Zahra was relieved that the raised scars confirmed she was indeed back.

John's warm breath hitched, and his body tensed. "Tell me I'm not dreaming this."

Zahra placed her hand on John's bicep and said, *"Not unless I'm dreaming this too, my love."*

She'd expected him to jump up or show a sense of excitement. His heart rate increased, but other than that, he lifted his arm away and hovered above her in tears. Zahra was concerned something was seriously wrong until John asked, "Are you in any pain?" His voice cracked as he spoke.

Zahra did a quick check, and other than being stiff, undoubtedly from lying still for so long, she felt fine. *"No, just stiff."*

That seemed to spur the big guy into action. John knelt on the bed and lifted Zahra into his arms. "Thank the gods. Thank you to whichever god sent you back to me. I would offer my prayers if I knew who they were."

"That would be the Goddess Mut," Zahra replied as she snuggled deeper into her mate's broad chest. How she'd missed this. *"But don't go praying to any one of those five, they're huge pains in my ass."* Zahra swore she could hear them laughing.

John pulled back to look her in the eyes. "Five Goddesses?"

"Yes. Hathor, Mut, Wadjet, Bastet, and the queen bitch, Sekhmet, all the Eyes of Ra." John seemed to pale. *"Can we discuss this later, please? I don't want to talk about them right now. I want to*

concentrate on being here with you. I've missed you so much. Had I known that time moved differently in other realms, I would have blown up a few of those pillars in Karnak, that's for sure." John tilted his head, and Zahra knew she wasn't making sense. She wanted him to know everything, but the fear of knowing what was to come and her duty to the entire world was overwhelming. Right now, she wanted to enjoy the simple pleasure of being in his arms.

John understood, as she knew he would. "There is plenty of time to talk things over later. You are all that's important to me."

She could feel the love pouring off her beleaguered mate. After everything she'd already put him through, he had stood by her side through it all and loved her all the more with every new day. The power she'd been given didn't compare to the gift of her mate. Nothing would ever shine as brightly as John.

"I love you," Zahra said as she tried to blink away the tears. *"I couldn't survive without you. Please, swear never to leave me no matter how much shit I put you through."*

"I'm not going anywhere that you are not, Zahra," John swore as he gently brushed away a few of her tears with the pad of his thumb. "You've not put me through anything I don't want in the first place, because it's the real you. Now let's get into a hot bath to help with those stiff muscles of yours, if you feel up to it."

She nodded her head and looked around for the bathroom door. *"Where are we?"* This wasn't her room, she couldn't scent the typical smells of the clan house, and there appeared to be no windows.

"We've moved into the bunker complex beneath our lands. Everyone has been evacuated into our protected facility." The sadness she felt coming from her mate when he explained the loss of their homes shook her to her core.

Though her own pack reminded her of worse times, there was still a connection to the land. She couldn't imagine the pain at being forced to abandon your entire past, especially when it was filled with happy, loving memories.

Her breath caught in her throat. Whatever happened while she was unconscious had to be severe enough to drive them underground. Zahra may have not been entirely ready to talk about what she'd learned, but that didn't mean she didn't want to know what her mate had been through.

"Tell me as much as you can, please."

***

Zahra sat leaning back against his chest in the hot, soapy water, as John began explaining the news of the last ten days. He wanted to protect her, but she had to have the details in case there was anything that could be relevant to her new status.

From the lives she'd saved ten days ago, to the return of the collector demons, and the battles that ensued and were still raging even now, he explained the subtle differences in these new hosts from their previous encounters with the evil demons. Their larger black eyes and a feel of consciousness instead of blind rage, to the slower rate of decomposition of host bodies.

The Porda Clan and North Woods Pack were safe, as well as many other shifter groups scattered around the world who'd been prepared for a hostile attack. Unfortunately, not all shifters would be spared, no matter how many the clan and pack took in. For now, most of their kind would be hunkering down, waiting for the violence to slow before venturing back out.

John gently rubbed the soapy loofah over his mate's shoulders and back. Thankful it didn't appear as though she'd lost any weight due to the length of time she'd been unconscious, but with her moving around now, John could get a much better look.

"The battles have been reduced to street level only? Where are the authorities?"

"Once the leaders of the human governments became infected, and the military turned on themselves, any joint efforts ended, resulting in an every-man-for-himself attitude," John explained. "I'll show you the reports tomorrow. They will help get you up to speed with the situation."

Instead, Zahra held up her hand. *"Can I see this from your memories, please? That will be the quickest way."*

"Are you sure?" John was hesitant, considering Zahra had only woken a little over an hour ago. "Things are bad out there. Can it wait until the morning?" He wanted this one bubble of peace and happiness to last a bit longer.

Zahra thought about it for a moment before answering, *"Yes, it can wait for morning. Now is for us, alone."*

"Thank you." John didn't want to keep anything from his mate. However, after ten days of indescribable fear and loss, John wanted to shut out the world if only for the rest of the night and concentrate on Zahra. With all that had already happened since finding his mate, their private time had been even more limited than typical fated mates.

His beautiful mate turned around in the tub to face him. *"When I saw you being taken down by that group of hosts, I thought I was going to lose you."*

"Takes a lot to keep this old bear down. Please, don't worry. I've trained my warriors to understand that someone, someday will force them to the ground. The only thing that matters is how fast you get back up before they have time to do any serious damage. I was back up within seconds."

"It's been a long time since I've had someone to fight for and to worry over. I'd forgotten how strong those feelings are and how crippling they can be. I love you, my big bear, and I want to spend every single day by your side."

John couldn't help but reach out and cup Zahra's rosy cheek. Her black hair with its one white streak hung down in waves fanning out around her while dipping beneath the water. She looked at him with such love that he thanked the Goddess Mut for returning her to him, even if she was a pain in Zahra's ass. Next time if they took his mate to have a discussion, they'd better take him as well.

"I love you, now and always, no matter what comes." John's need to have her even closer took over, and he lifted her up onto his lap before diving in for a deep, pleasure-filled kiss. They'd never had time to enjoy and explore each other. Now that would change. John wanted to express his love for Zahra through his body, along with his words.

Their tongues dueled as each explored thoroughly before being forced to break apart to breathe. The feel of his mate's soft skin gliding over his own made his heart race. Her soft moans would have brought John to his knees if he weren't already sitting in the tub.

She wrapped her long legs around his waist and slid her body flush with his. Even with him being three times her size, she was the one in control of how far this went.

Zahra ran her nails through his short hair, eliciting a husky growl from deep inside his chest. Bears were tactile creatures, and with every scrape of her nails or brush of her teeth over his overheated skin, his need grew like a wildfire.

The test of his resolve came when Zahra licked and nibbled her way up the side of his neck on her way to suck on his earlobe. "Zahra, love, I'm trying to keep control over myself, but if you keep this up, it will soon break."

She stopped mid-lick and looked at him, confusion written all over her face. *"You don't want to make love?"*

"Of course I do." He clamped his hands on her upper arms before she could pull away. "That isn't what I meant. I want to make love to you, but I didn't want to rush you. You haven't indicated that you wanted more…to be fully mated. Besides, you're still recovering."

Zahra's confusion disappeared, and her body relaxed against him. *"I've been giving you mixed messages from the start, haven't I?"*

"I understand. It's been a tumultuous time for you, having so much thrown your way." He didn't want her to feel guilty for something she had no control over. "First, a bunch of strangers show up on your land, then you find Rose returning after so long, and then a fated mate is thrown into the mix. I'm surprised and so grateful you didn't take off when it all came to a head."

"You still want me, even with these?" She held up her hands, presenting her new markings as if the sight of them should be terrifying. *"I'm sure this is going to cause even more trouble."*

"I could never not want you. I love you, and no matter what you tell me about what these are or where it's leading us, I will always love you."

The smile returned to her face before she said, *"Then make love to me."*

He didn't have to be asked twice. He stood in the tub with Zahra safely in his arms and stepped out onto the thick mat. At first, he thought to carry her over to their bed, but worried the wet sheets might make his mate cold later in the evening. So he grabbed a big white towel before heading to the other room where he proceeded to dry her from head to toe.

Her gaze followed his every move, and her beautiful smile assured him of her happiness. *"Of course I'm happy. I'm with the man I love who is so concerned with my comfort that he power-dried me."*

John could feel his cheeks getting warm. "Too big of a hurry? Was I too rough?"

She slid herself onto their bed and laid her head down on one of his pillows. Her long hair gathered around her, soft and silky, begging to be touched. "You are never too rough with me, bear. Now get over here."

The bed groaned when he crawled onto it and hovered over Zahra. With their bodies only inches apart, John lowered his head and ran the tip of his tongue down her neck, stopping several times to lick and bite but never breaking the skin. That would be reserved for their mating bites, which each would give to one another while they made love.

Her soft cries and moans echoed in his head and spurred him on. She tasted so sweet, and his greedy bear would have continued licking every inch of her smooth skin, but became distracted by her swollen nipples.

Change of plan. John sucked one into his mouth and flicked the hard nubbin with his tongue, causing Zahra's back to rise off the bed. He could feel her nails on the back of his head, holding him in place, and grinned inwardly as he doubled down and rolled her other nipple between his thumb and index finger.

The sound of tearing sheets had him looking up to find her canines peeking out from below her top lip as she watched him with her glowing eyes. The claws of her free hand had a firm hold on the sheets and mattress.

His mate couldn't have given him a better compliment than to know how much pleasure he was giving her. Zahra's hips bucked up, and she rubbed herself against his thigh, creating friction against her hot, wet core.

John adjusted his body to Zahra's side, never once releasing the hold he had on her nipple with his mouth. He ghosted his other hand over her quivering stomach and didn't stop until his fingers were carding through her thick, springy hair and moved onto her wet folds. His moan followed hers.

There was no need for words. They were inside each other's minds, hearts, and souls. Sharing every touch and emotion as only mates could. He slid his finger inside her while reaching for her clit with his thumb. Her body bowed up off the bed, her mouth open and gasping.

With his lips, tongue, and fingers, he brought his beloved mate to the edge of orgasm multiple times. Until the words *please* and *need* floated through his mind, and he was more than happy to oblige.

Pumping two of his fingers deep while squeezing her swollen clit was precisely what she needed, and pleasure raced through her body and into his, making him fight to stave off his own orgasm.

Before Zahra had a chance to come down from her high, John repositioned himself between her trembling legs and waited until her gaze cleared. "Ready, love?"

She wrapped her arms around his neck and smiled wide with her canines extended. *"Yes. I want nothing more than to be fully mated to you."*

He lowered his head and took her lips in a slow, easy kiss while he pressed the head of his cock to her tight core and pushed forward until his balls lay flush against her skin. The silky feel of his mate's body squeezing around him had his body throbbing for release. She wrapped her legs around his waist after the first couple of thrusts.

Every touch, moan, and squeeze of her muscles drew him higher. Her nails dug into his back, and he growled his approval. He wanted his mate delirious with pleasure, and by the look of her unfocused gaze, he was succeeding.

Their bodies moved together, and with no mental or physical barriers left between them, they joined as one. As her body began tensing, he knew she was getting closer to her second orgasm.

He broke their kiss and looked down at his beautiful mate. "I love you, Zahra. I swear this life, and all the others, to you."

"I love you, John. I swear everything that I am to you, in this life and all others."

He returned to kissing his way down her neck and stopped to lick the spot on her shoulder that would bear his mark. His canines extended to full length before he struck, sinking his teeth into her soft flesh. She exploded around him as she came moments before burying her teeth into his neck.

A freight train of need rushed through his body, whisking away reality from and around them. By the time his muscles released, John felt as if his body had been turned inside out, and he melted down onto his mate. He rolled their bodies, placing her on top.

For several minutes both lazily licked at each other's mating bites, basking in their love. Their bond was strengthening even further, if that were possible. Their DNA now flowed in each other's veins, connecting them as nothing else possibly could.

When he heard Zahra's breathing evening out, he pulled the blankets up to cover them. Tomorrow would come fast enough, and he imagined it would be a day filled with new hopes and burdens. Getting used to this new way of life while trying to figure out what came next would be one of their many concerns.

The only thing John was sure of, other than his love for his mate, was that whatever the other Eyes of Ra had discussed with Zahra was going to add a new twist to this whole situation.

Whether it was for the good, they'd have to wait to find out.

Chapter Eight

"So, we have to go out and find these humans?"

"Yes." Zahra could understand the confusion on Mason's face as he asked.

"And protect them?" Riker added.

"Yes, again." This wasn't going well.

"Humans killed our parents," Jewel stated the obvious. "And we have to save them?"

"Not all humans are like the hunters," Marie said while bringing more carafes of coffee into the large boardroom. Both Porda Clan and North Woods Pack leaders were in attendance, among others.

Zahra had already shared the events of her meeting with the other goddesses chosen as the Eyes of Ra. After everyone's shock wore off, and most had stopped staring at her hands, they were beginning to try to come up with a plan of sorts.

"Yes, but how do we know which is which? What will be the identifier between a shifter-killing human and a less deadly one?" Rose asked, and Zahra knew she was doing her job as matriarch, trying to protect their people. "I agree with Marie, there are some good and bad humans, the same as shifters, but how do we know who's who?"

"All I have to go on is a vague assurance that I will know. I can relay that information instantly through the links, but anything specific is more of a wait-and-see kind of thing. I'll know when I see one." For now, that would have to be enough.

"What about the children and babies?" Marie asked while standing in the back of the room. Zahra had noticed she refused to be front and center no matter where she was.

"We hadn't thought about that," Riker admitted. "In essence, they would be among the last humans to be infected, if at all. The young are pure of heart and soul. How do we save them, and what happens when they grow up and turn on us?"

The room fell into silence, each one of them looking equally puzzled. Zahra wasn't sure how they'd missed something so dire. Of course, they'd been busy ensuring their own people's safety, but now that had been in motion, odd circumstances they hadn't prepared for were bound to pop up.

"Well, no one is going aboveground until it quiets down out there," Axel announced.

"Agreed," Mason said. "This will give us all the time needed to get settled into our new living situation and come up with a more concrete plan."

"All entrances have been secured and sealed," John explained from Zahra's side. "Nothing will be coming through them. All sensors set up throughout both territories are functioning as expected and sending data twenty-four seven. Xander and I have set up joint security monitors with twenty-four-hour staffing, as well as amalgamated forces to run security sweeps in shifts throughout both facilities."

"The underground river is producing enough hydroelectricity to keep the day-to-day operations working without having to draw on any battery reserves," Xander said before smiling wide, confusing Zahra, until one of the doors opened.

Raz walked in with a tiny bundle in her arms. The baby had been asleep earlier when the meeting first began, explaining why Raz hadn't arrived until now. However, knowing her mates, Raz had been kept up to date.

Until now, Zahra hadn't had the chance to spend time with the new arrival considering she had become conscious only late last night.

Axel and Xander stood and went to Raz's side, kissing her and the baby. Raz and her mates then walked around the table and toward Zahra, who was on her feet before they reached her. She couldn't help her excitement at seeing the little girl healthy and happy. It would help wash away the memories of how Zahra found her the day she was born.

"Zahra, I'd like you to meet Asta," Raz said as she held out the multicolored bundle of blankets to Zahra's waiting arms.

A tuft of orange and blonde hair stuck up from the center of the bundle. Zahra used her fingers to move the coverings aside to find a pair of the most vibrant azure eyes staring back up at her. Asta was perfect. Everything that was right in this world was contained in this little bundle, and Zahra couldn't stop her tears from falling.

Both Raz and Rose placed their hands on hers over top of baby Asta, and all three of their goddess markings began to glow in unison. The light from Zahra's hands and Rose and Raz's filigree facial markings merged together over the precious baby in protection.

Raz looked up at Zahra, her eyes tinged gold the same as Rose's, and more than likely her own, and said, "Welcome, sister."

***

"I guess this means goddesses don't have to necessarily be alphas," Marie commented while setting a tray of cheese and crackers on the small table between them.

Zahra was still feeling a bit weak after this morning's meeting where she'd had to share everything, hear what had been going on, explain that they had to find the "right" humans, oh, and save the world twelve hours after she'd been returned to her body. She'd decided to return to their rooms and run through video footage and reports from the last two days, while John continued with his duties of protecting the clan.

Considering everything her mate had explained to her, including what television was, Zahra had a good understanding of how to use the remote. She'd pointed it at the TV hanging on the wall in the small living room and kitchen area of their living space, pressed the red power button, and was happy to discover that she'd been able to pick up new things quickly, which had helped since she had so much to learn.

"I guess not," she answered Marie, *"because there is no way I'm an alpha wolf."* She looked at her constant companion. *"You know you don't have to stay with me now that I'm awake. I appreciate everything you've done for me, but if you have other obligations, I'll understand."*

"Oh," Marie said as she stopped herself from sitting in the other chair. "If you'd prefer to be alone, I can leave."

"No, no, I don't want you to leave. I didn't want you to feel forced to watch over me if you had other things on your plate today."

Marie sat down in the chair. "I like the company if you don't mind. Makes the day pass faster, and I'm not as lonely."

Zahra turned all her attention on Marie and put the video on mute. *"Does anyone stay with you? Friends, distant relatives who didn't have anything to do with your parents' plans?"*

Marie looked away before answering, "No roommate. My immediate family, as you know, are all gone, and the few distant ones still among the clan refuse to speak with me. They don't want to be associated with what my parents tried to do. My friends, understandably, want nothing to do with me after what I've done. I can't blame them."

Zahra wanted to rage against the cruelty of it, but a part of her understood the others being wary of the woman who'd tried to overthrow Rose as the matriarch. Anger wouldn't help this situation, and the easy acceptance with which Marie took the blame told Zahra that Marie wouldn't listen to the many reasons this wasn't her fault.

"Where's your private room?"

"Two levels below this one."

"Are there any open rooms on this level?"

"Yes. Most of the rooms around yours are still empty," Marie explained. "No one wanted to disturb the general while he watched over you, so the area was kept quiet."

"Good," Zahra said, making Marie look at her strangely. *"Not the fact of John suffering, but that we can easily move you into the rooms next to ours."*

"Why would you do that?"

"Simple. I like you, and we get along well. It would be nice to have a friend nearby. Remember, I'm new here."

"But associating with me regularly won't help endear you to the others," Marie explained.

"Don't really care about that. If they choose not to accept me because you are my friend, then perhaps they weren't someone I'd want to be friends with in the first place."

Marie looked unsure, so Zahra took the heat off her. *"You don't have to decide now. The offer is on the table whenever you want to take it."*

She smiled before nodding, indicating that she'd think about it. Zahra accepted this, knowing she'd have Marie moved up the moment she agreed. It would probably be best if Zahra mentioned it to John so that a room remained empty, and she made a mental note to tell him tonight.

She and Marie turned back to the television, and she unmuted the sound. All joy at having a potential friend nearby vanished as the scenes of destruction played out in front of her. News stations had gone off the air days earlier, radio stations days before that, and now they were only receiving reports from shifters located all over the world. The clan and pack were sharing the same in return, hoping there would be some way to assist one another through this carnage.

Rose had mentioned something about a satellite, which, as far as she understood, was a machine in space, keeping the groups connected. Apparently, a wealthy Russian bear shifter had sent it up during something called the Cold War in case the humans pushed some sort of button. Zahra hadn't made it that far in her studies yet.

Rose had explained that they lived in Oregon and had given her a globe so that Zahra had a better idea of where everyone was located, which helped immensely.

They watched burning buildings crash to the ground, with no police or fire personnel in sight. In fact, Zahra could make out a few squad cars in the background empty with their doors hanging open. Her stomach churned as the commentary of what they were seeing flashed across the bottom of the screen. It mentioned a fire burning at a Staples Center, wherever that was.

The picture changed, and Zahra recognized a structure in the background. The Eiffel Tower stood watch over the burning city of Paris below. This camera had to have been installed high above the buildings to catch such an expansive view. She could see movement down on the ground near the fountains of Trocadero Gardens, but they were too far away to make out if they were hosts or humans.

"I've heard that a North Korean military unit turned their guns on the people in small villages throughout Southeast Asia. They seem to be much more organized than before," Marie said while she picked up her glass of water with a shaky hand.

The video flipped again, and this time, they had a much closer view of the street level. According to the shifter commentator, they were now seeing London, England. The streets were empty of people, car doors stood open, and a few still had their lights on.

Food carts lay tipped over on the ground with the odd cat standing by devouring a leisurely lunch. Zahra had been told animals couldn't become infected, and she wondered if that was for the same reason shifters couldn't be, considering they share themselves with their animals.

It wasn't long before movement caught Zahra's attention on the right side of the screen. Two hosts, with their large black eyes scanning the area, walked out from behind a delivery truck with rifles in their hands. Seeing them made Zahra's skin crawl, but there seemed to be a difference between these hosts and the ones she'd fought only ten days ago.

Their previous jerky movements and lack of control over their hosts' bodies had now smoothed out to the point that they moved much like normal humans. She could make out a bit of decomposition around the joints but nothing compared to the pieces of flesh that had been falling off their bones days earlier.

They were also communicating with each other, which Zahra had never seen them do before. *"They're talking to one another?"*

"Yes, that's a new development. It seems that the longer this goes on, the more the demons learn about how to control their hosts." John's voice came from the open doorway leading out into the hall, startling them. "I didn't mean to scare you ladies, but I felt your confusion and anger, Zahra."

He shut the door and walked over to her. With his strong arms, he lifted her so that he could sit in the chair with her on his lap. She didn't mind in the least. She could use those big arms around her right about now watching their new reality unfold before them.

"So they're sentient? There isn't one demon controlling them all?"

"In a way, yes. They seem to have changed their perception of the hosts. Where before the demons didn't care how they treated the bodies, if it fell apart, they would simply move on to another one."

"Maybe they're figuring out there are benefits to having a working body," Marie suggested.

"Like driving a vehicle and using weapons accurately."

"Exactly," he agreed. "However, it also appears they can't retain the host's more intricate or specialized memories."

"How do you know?" Zahra asked.

"When the military was first called out to help during the initial attacks, their airplanes and helicopters dropped out of the sky once the pilots were infected," John explained. "Then again, as you can see, they can learn basic knowledge, like how to fire a gun."

"It's good to know that they can't move globally and are pretty much stuck on their own continent. However, it seems that this time around, they don't want to destroy humans but become them."

That was a scary thought. Action on the screen brought Zahra back to the streets of London. The two hosts must have heard something because they were both taking cover behind the truck. Sure enough, a girl no more than six years old came limping out from a side street.

"No, no, no," Zahra chanted, but it was too late; the hosts had already seen her and were approaching. Their toothy grins sent chills down Zahra's spine. The little girl saw them and froze to the spot where she stood in the middle of the street. She didn't care if this was a human child or not.

John's arms tightened around her, and before she could think of anything she could do to stop the hosts from killing the child, a large SUV came speeding around the corner and ran the two hosts down using the large push bars on the front grill. The vehicle came to a stop beside the girl, and the driver's door opened, allowing a large man dressed in what looked like a police uniform to step out.

He went to his knees in front of the child and said something they couldn't hear. Soon she took his hand, and he helped her up into the SUV. Before getting back into the driver's seat himself, the man turned around to scan the area.

Zahra's heart stopped, and for a split second, she thought she was going to pass out.

"Mate, what's wrong?" John asked, having felt her shock and distress.

"We have to go there." Zahra felt a bit numb.

"To London, England?" Her mate's voice sounded strangled.

Marie leaned over the small table to take Zahra's now shaking hand. "Why?"

"Because I think I've found our first rescue."

"The little girl?" John asked.

"No, the police officer. He has shifter DNA in his body, I'm sure of it."

"Well, shit. We're going to London," John said, and the fact that he didn't question her felt amazing. For the first time, Zahra didn't have to prove herself. She had been believed.

Chapter Nine

John held on to his mate's hand as they turned down another corridor. While they waited for the alpha triads to come back to them with their decision on whether to teleport to London, he'd decided to show Zahra around the facility. He'd also hoped to take her mind off what needed to be done if they were to rescue the officer.

Obviously, whoever this guy was, he was going around saving people, which would mean when the clan found him, he wouldn't be alone. No one could come up with what to do if other humans were there. Did they bring any children with them and leave the other adults behind because they could be a danger or could be infected?

No one had the answers. Any way they examined it, someone was going to lose.

As they wandered, numerous shifters came up to Zahra to thank her for saving their lives or that of a loved one the day of the attack on the North Woods Pack. As always, she was gracious and played down her part in the whole thing, even though all knew many would have died that day if not for her.

"Have I told you how much I love you today?" he asked.

She stopped walking and turned to look up at him. Her smile was genuine and always made him feel loved.

"I'm sure you have, but I won't tire of hearing you repeat it." Her saucy grin worked wonders on his soul.

John cupped Zahra's smooth cheeks in the palms of his hands. Her blue eyes seemed to sparkle more than the overhead lighting could account for. Stunning. *Mine.*

"You make this old bear dream of things I never imagined to be possible before you came into my life. You're my heart. I'm sure it couldn't beat without you. I love you, my mate."

Zahra stood on the tips of her toes, requesting a kiss that John was all too willing to give. Her soft lips opened, allowing him entrance as their tongues dueled. He lifted her off the ground and into his arms, ensuring she didn't have to strain her neck up to kiss him. John would do everything in his power to prevent his mate from any pain.

"Do you two ever come up for air?" a familiar voice teased from behind them.

"Good morning, Jewel," he replied after setting Zahra back on her feet.

"Hello, Jewel." Zahra's rosy cheeks made his stomach flip as she welcomed the clan doctor.

The doctor laughed and pointed at the infirmary sign above a nearby door. "What's brought you two down to my neck of the woods?" Jewel looked at Zahra when she asked, "Are you unwell?" Doc was much like her brothers, Mason and Riker, always concerned with the health of the clan and ready to help at a moment's notice. If shifters were to face the end of civilization, he would prefer to face it among his clan.

"I'm feeling great," Zahra confirmed. *"John was giving me a tour around, hoping I don't manage to get myself lost as often as I've already done."*

"Ah, good idea," Jewel agreed. "And now that you know where I'll be lurking, feel free to come by anytime, sick or not."

"I will, but do bears lurk?" Zahra teased back.

John couldn't help but laugh. "Thank you, Jewel."

Once the doc returned to her clinic, John wrapped his arm around his mate and carried on with his tour. They visited the central kitchen and communal dining areas. Even though each private room had its own modest kitchen, shifters enjoyed the feeling of community and often preferred to eat together.

The same thing applied to the large common areas built explicitly for the clan and pack so they could come together whenever they wished. During stressful times, shifters sought the comfort of one another. Like the big family they were. Their bonds would grow between the two groups, as they became something new.

John guided Zahra from clan territory over to pack lands and back. Merging their two forces only made sense. The two groups of shifters had been allies for centuries, and John respected the wolves and their alpha triad. They were reliable, caring, honest, and loyal.

Either group would help the other when in need, as they had done only weeks ago.

"How long do you think we'll have to live down here?" Zahra asked.

"I'm not sure, love," John replied. "Worst-case scenario, we'll never be able to return to safely living aboveground. However, I don't think that will be the case. At best, right now, we're operating on the belief that we might have to stay down here for one or two years at most."

Her face paled. *"I want our children to be able to feel the sun on their faces and to know what it feels like to race through the forest and swim in a lake."*

He wrapped his arms around her and pulled her close. They were standing in the middle of a shared space covered in soft rugs, cushions, and blankets, along with couches and chairs. John moved them over to a corner filled with extra-large cushions and cuddled her in the luxurious sanctuary.

"I want the same, love. Our mission is to make this world safe for them. It'll take time, but our conviction is strong; we'll never give up, no matter what happens."

"Yes, no matter what happens."

***

"So a quick in and out?"

"Yes, once we find him, we're leaving," Zahra confirmed with her mate once more. She understood he was worried about her safety, and she loved him for it, but they had to take this chance before a host got off a lucky shot and took the guy out.

They were taking a small group along with them to search for the human-shifter so they could teleport more easily and risk fewer lives. Naturally, Zahra and John were going, as well as Marie, who'd appointed herself Zahra's wing-woman. Riker, Xander, and Rose would be joining them since Zahra hadn't been able to get her own powers under control and didn't fancy teleporting them into a wall. Warriors and enforcers rounded out the group.

It had been decided that both alphas would stay behind. Now was not the time to risk leaving their people leaderless. Raz, understandably, would be remaining as well to care for Asta and protect the clan. Altogether, they were a group of ten, and other than the videos, none of them knew what to expect when they got to London.

Their group stood assembled in the main boardroom. Most were heavily armed, except for Rose and Zahra, who both had been given powers to protect themselves better than any man-made weapon ever could. Everyone was wearing black tactical gear emblazoned with the universally known symbol for a medic on all sides.

Their theory was simple: surviving humans might not shoot at them as quickly if they thought they were there to help. It really didn't matter what the hosts thought. They'd attack no matter what they were wearing.

The triads had decided to bring back any young children, if possible. However, anyone older would have to be viewed on a case-by-case basis with Rose at the ready to suck a demon out of a host at the slightest provocation. They'd already cleared an entire level in the complex to house the rescues, not knowing how many were expected. Raz, the reincarnated warrior goddess Avra, verified that she'd been guaranteed that once the humans were safely inside the complex, they could no longer be infected. The collector demons couldn't pass the wards that had been placed over the facility.

The more powerful gods hadn't thought to create wards because they hadn't taken the demon threat seriously until lesser goddesses had stepped in and began helping the shifters. Zahra suspected they realized that without life on earth, there would be no one left to bask in their glory, write stories about them, or pray to them and leave offerings.

Usually, Zahra wasn't a cynic—okay, maybe after everything she'd been through, she might be—but her feet were planted firmly in reality. No worshippers equated to no gods.

However, that still left the fact that they would have humans in their midst, along with a large group of shifters who had all been touched by the evil of the hunters. It was a powder keg ready to blow, but they had no other choice but to watch the fireworks when they went off.

If Zahra hadn't taken Ra's offer, the people she'd met from clan and pack would more than likely be dead, and most certainly, Asta would have never had a chance at life.

"Ready?" John asked as he checked to make sure each of her red medic symbols were completely visible.

"Yes, I'm ready," she confirmed before sending all her love across their private link. *"Don't worry. We shifters are tough to take down."*

"If that's supposed to make me feel better, baby, it didn't work. Stay close to me, please."

"I don't plan on being anywhere else." Zahra wrapped her arms around her mate's neck and kissed him. If her entire existence had led up to this, then she regretted nothing.

Raz held Asta in her arms while Axel held her. Xander hugged his brother, kissed Raz and Asta before joining the group. Mason hugged Riker before lifting Rose into the air to kiss her.

"You keep a watch on our mate, little brother, or there's going to be hell to pay," Mason warned.

Rose slapped Mason on his chest and said, "I can take care of myself, don't be an overbearing bear."

The group laughed, easing the tension somewhat, for which Zahra was thankful.

"Okay, gear up. Let's get ready to go," John ordered the warriors. "Sooner we get this over with the better."

Zahra reached for John's hand while the warriors linked their arms. This was it. Now she would find out what she'd signed up for. For a moment, she couldn't help but think back over all the things that had happened to her in such a short period of time.

Lesson learned. Next time, she'd be more specific about what she wished for. Sure, she'd hoped for company to end her loneliness and isolation, but becoming the Eye and fighting in a collector demon end-of-the-world war hadn't been anywhere on her list.

She squeezed her mate's hand tighter, and he looked down at her with a warm smile. Who was she kidding? Zahra would do it all again to be standing by John's side.

Rose held on to Riker, and her goddess markings began to glow in preparation for the jump. Zahra looked down to find her symbols for the Eye of Ra glowing as well. She might not have mastered her powers yet, but she was learning, and it was good to know those powers were waiting for her to figure her shit out.

Electricity arched through the room seconds before her feet left the ground. A strong wind whipped around them at the same time as she felt the first drops of water. Once she felt a hard surface beneath her, she realized they'd landed in the middle of a severe rainstorm.

"Guess it's called rainy London for a reason," Marie whispered as she moved in behind Zahra, gun at the ready.

The sky was gray and cloudy, and the rain was falling in sheets, but the one thing that Zahra noticed above all else was how deathly quiet the city was. Sure enough, they were in the exact spot where they'd seen the human save the girl. The hosts' bodies were still decomposing over by the sidewalk where they'd been run down. Which brought on more questions, such as why the hosts hadn't returned to dust on their deaths. Another mystery left for another time.

It had to be midafternoon, but the weather covered everything in a dreary haze. Buildings stood empty on either side of the street, with only the occasional light between the shards of broken glass. Several rooms had undeniable hand-shaped red streaks across the walls, while the blood coating the street had long since washed away in the rain.

Their team hunkered down under a tractor-trailer to wait for their shifter contacts in the area. A clowder of lynx living nearby had been monitoring the police officer until their team was able to get to London.

Zahra sensed two figures nearing from the east. Their gaits were staggered, as if they might be drunk. Great. Warriors spread out to cover the area, leaving her, John, Marie, Rose, Xander, and Riker to wait for the lynx to show up. As the figures neared, Zahra could easily make out their scents, feline, and strangely enough something smoky.

"Marijuana," John explained. *Weird.* With shifters' heightened senses, smoking would be like sucking on a burnt timber just taken out of the fire.

She watched as the two slowly rounded a black, four-door car lying on its driver's side on the nearby sidewalk. The two scanned the area around them before coming closer. Warriors appeared out of the darkness to surround them.

"Bloody tosser. You asked for our help, din'ya?" the taller of the two lynx shifters whispered with a low growl. Zahra couldn't miss the slight shake in his hands.

"That's why they aren't pointing their guns at you," Xander explained as they moved out from under the trailer and joined the two arrivals.

"Let's get this over with before one of them black-eyed fuckers comes along," the second lynx shifter said as he rechecked the area. "I ain't getting killed over no human bag o' shite."

"We only asked for you to show us where he is. Once you do, you are free to go on your way," Ricker explained, never taking his eyes off the lynx.

"Do you have what we agreed upon?" the same shifter asked while licking his lips.

"Yes," John answered, holding out a small bag. He opened it to reveal gold coins.

Zahra remembered when her mate had explained to her that the currency of today would be worthless once governments began to fall. He'd been right, though she'd never doubted him. The taller one took the bag and shoved it into the inside pocket of his coat, his eyes shifting from side to side.

"Right then, let's go get this meat puppet for you," the lynx said as he pulled his trousers up over his protruding belly.

"Charming," Zahra remarked, making the two men look around to find out who had spoken, considering she hadn't moved her lips. *"Over here, gentlemen. And I use that term loosely."*

The shorter lynx shifter looked over at Zahra and asked, "That you talking? My clowder doesn't have a link with any of you, so how did we hear you?" Then he glanced down at her throat and grimaced. "Oh, cause you ain't got no voice. Serious minging, that is."

Zahra had no idea what he had said, but whatever it was, it had several people moving at once. Marie and Rose moved closer while John stood directly in front of her. She had to peek around her big bear to see what was going on.

"Okay, okay, keep your bloody hands to yourself," the man who'd spoken to her said as he and his friend found themselves in a warrior's chokehold.

"I can retrieve the information on this guy's location from their memories. They won't even have to come along," Rose offered.

But Zahra still wanted to know what he'd said. *"What did he mean, minging?"*

John turned slightly to look down at her. "It's nothing. He's a foul-mouthed asshole."

"It means that neck of yours is gross…it's disgusting, doggy. Maybe you should cov—" Whatever else the lynx shifter was about to say was cut off by John's hand closing around his throat.

"Your leader isn't going to be happy with you two assholes," Xander warned. "Little kitties like yourself shouldn't be playing with bears and wolves, you might get hurt."

"Wait…are either of you drunk or high?" Zahra had to ask. *"Or are you usually idiots?"*

"None a-ya can touch us. We got the information you Yanks need. So the price has just gone up." The tall one sneered at them, which was funny considering the arm around his throat kept tightening, making his last few words nothing more than a strangled squeak.

"Okay. Vote's in, you're stupid. That's the problem here," Zahra concluded while walking out from behind John, who growled his displeasure. *"Shifters are in a battle for survival, and you two yahoos think it's time for games and deals. Here's a deal for you, which one of you kind gentlemen wishes to die first?"*

"Wait—wait. What?"

"Your first mistake was underestimating how important this mission is to us. Second, that I give a rat's ass what you two flaming idiots think of my scars. Your last and maybe biggest mistake was not listening. I'm sure your brilliant minds were too busy making plans of how to spend the money to hear what my matriarch had said."

Zahra was tired of people trying to use others to step over to get what they wanted. Sure, it stung to hear someone say nasty things about her, but after everything she'd been through, and the state of the world, she no longer cared what other people saw when they looked at her. She already had shifters who cared for her and loved her. Nothing these two bozos could say would ever matter.

"Said?" the short, foul-mouthed one asked.

Zahra's hands began to glow, and Rose stepped closer to her. They joined hands, setting off her friend's filigree markings, and they moved to within reach of the two now struggling men.

"Yes, the part where I mentioned taking your memories," Rose explained before raising her hand to the lynx shifter who had called Zahra that terrible name.

"You see, typically, Rose doesn't like to use this particular power given to her by the Goddess Thorne, but in your case, she'll make an exception."

"Goddesses don't exist, that bullshit is for the old-timers."

Idiots until the end. *"You should have learned to listen to your elders."* Zahra grinned. *"What a shame, when we need all the shifters we can get to work together for our survival."*

Rose lifted her hand and placed it on his head. He struggled for a moment before falling silent.

Chapter Ten

Twenty-five minutes later, their team of ten stood outside a brick cottage several miles away from the city. There were no lights or movement from inside, but John could sense three humans in there somewhere.

Their team had spread out around the property to get a better look. John was already receiving reports from the warriors of rudimentary traps and noisemakers set up to alert those dwelling inside to unexpected visitors. John remained with Zahra and Marie, while Rose went with Riker and Xander, the remainder of their party disappearing into the darkness.

Zahra hadn't left John's side, which calmed him and his bear, but what happened earlier still ate at him. His beautiful mate should never be forced to listen to shit like that. Those two lynx shifters were lucky John hadn't ripped out their tongues. They wouldn't have been able to grow that back.

However, his kindhearted mate wouldn't allow him to do that. So, John had taken it upon himself to teach them the errors of ways. They'd live.

In the process, he'd retrieved the gold coins they'd brought as payment. Arrangements were being made to ensure the leaders of the clowder received the coins since they could use the money, and they didn't deserve to suffer for those two idiots' plans.

"Are you okay?" John asked. She hadn't said a word since leaving those lynx behind.

"No, not really," she admitted.

"Don't listen to anything they said—" John began but was stopped by his mate.

"Not because of that, sweetheart." Zahra laid her small hand on his arm. *"I meant what I said, what they think or say no longer has an effect on me. I have you, and I'm stronger now. The thing that's worrying me is how many shifters are out there like those two lynx*

waiting to take advantage of somebody. How are we ever going to work together when you can't trust anyone?"

John took a moment to again thank the gods for bringing Zahra into his life. She always amazed him with her strength. Still more worried for others than herself. He placed his much larger hand over the top of hers. "I have to believe there are more shifters like you, my mate. That will give us the edge we need to make it through this."

Zahra kissed the back of his hand and snuggled closer. The warriors were busy dismantling the security measures around the cottage, at the same time discussing through their link the best ways to approach without turning this into a shooting gallery.

"We could try surprising them," one of the wolf enforcers suggested.

"No good. I bet the dude already knows we're here," Riker surmised.

"What about calling out to them, let them know we're here to help?" Marie asked.

"We don't want to risk any nearby demons hearing us," Xander said.

"Then what?" Rose asked.

"I'll have to walk up to the house unarmed so they can see I'm not one of the hosts. Then I can explain before anyone gets off a shot."

"No way in hell are you going out there unarmed and alone. The human could be crazy, or scared, and not give a shit what you say. He could shoot you before any of us could stop him." John wasn't willing to risk Zahra more than they already were doing. If Ra wanted the human-shifters so badly, he could come down here himself and save them. *"I hate to bring this up, but how would you communicate with a human?"*

"I'm sure you'll have your gun trained on him from back here. Anything goes wrong, feel free to step in." Zahra was trying to make an insane suggestion seem logical. John wasn't buying it. *"As for my voice, now that I can be heard out loud when I speak, as long as I wear something over my mouth so that they can't see that my mouth isn't moving, I should be fine."*

"It makes the most sense," Xander agreed.

"Zahra has a point," Riker seconded. *"She can use one of the medical masks from the kits."*

"This is what I've been chosen to do, find and rescue the human-shifters. If Ra wants them saved, hopefully he won't let his messenger die at the first chance we've had to try." Zahra seemed adamant about this plan, which made John crazy.

"Agreed, it's the best chance we have of no one getting hurt," Riker decided.

John tried to keep his growl out of the conversation but failed. *"How would you feel if it were your mate with the target on her?"*

"I completely understand, and if the two of you think it's too big of a risk, we'll figure out some other way," Rose mediated. No one wanted an angry bear on their hands right now.

John looked at his mate, pleading for her to change her mind. By the determined set of her jaw and her piercing blue eyes, John knew her decision had been made, and he wasn't going to like it.

"You will stay in my sights at all times. You are not to go into the cottage alone, no matter what the human says. If he even breathes at you the wrong way, I'll end him, Ra or not."

Zahra's gaze softened, and she wrapped her arms around his waist. *"Thank you for understanding. I have to try."*

"Yeah, well, you better let me win the next argument."

"Deal," Zahra agreed before leaning in for a kiss.

When they separated, John was all business. *"Okay, everyone, be alert to any possible threats. No one takes their eyes off Zahra, understand?"*

"I'll be back in no time," she assured before standing, placing the mask over her mouth, and turning toward the cottage.

"You'd better be," John responded and lined up the sights on his rifle. "There'll be hell to pay if you get a scratch."

"Yes, General." Zahra winked and took her first step out from behind the tree they were using for cover.

Every sense was on high alert, his muscles tight and at the ready, his focus unbreakable. No one was going to harm his mate.

***

What the hell was she thinking? Walking out into the open, expecting not to get shot. She might as well have a flashing sign over her head announcing her arrival.

Zahra could feel the eyes on her though she saw no one even with her enhanced eyesight. She still didn't know if one set belonged to the rescue guy inside the cottage. She raised her hands out to her sides so that everyone could see she was unarmed. The one positive: the rain had stopped.

She could feel her mate's intensity through their link. John was honed in on her and her alone. Zahra loved her mate and understood his feeling about this plan, however, she'd been chosen as the Eye, and it was her responsibility to rescue as many human-shifters as she could. She hoped it didn't get her killed before she'd even gotten started.

"You can stop right there and turn around. I have nothing here for you," a deep voice echoed around her.

Zahra stopped walking but kept her arms out to her sides. She noticed that the man didn't have a British accent. *"My name is Zahra. I've come to help."* She even made the extra effort of moving her lips beneath the mask so that nothing seemed out of the ordinary.

"You're not British."

"Neither are you. We're from Oregon."

"We?"

"Please, don't even try to pretend you didn't already know that." Zahra figured the guy would prefer straight and to the point right about now. *"We saw you save the little girl and came to help before the demons show up."*

"Demons?"

"Yeah, the messed-up, black-eyed creatures that used to be human. Occasionally leave a body part lying around."

"How did you see me? I scanned the area and saw no one."

"We have a lot of sensors set up around the city," Zahra explained.

"Are you military?"

"More like Special Forces." They were special, all right. *"I don't mean to pressure you, but we're not sure when those creepy assholes are going to show up. Can we come talk to you, please?"*

Zahra waited as the human thought it through. Maybe this wasn't the best plan.

"Okay, but only you."

Zahra could hear John's growl ringing through the link. *"I understand your apprehension at allowing us near you and the people you are protecting, but my...husband made me swear not to go inside alone."*

"Your husband let you walk out here alone with all the shit going on?" the man asked in disbelief.

"My husband is well aware that I can take care of myself, thank you."

Before the human could answer, a small cry sounded from inside the cottage.

"Do you have any food and medicine?" he asked.

"Yes, full medical and enough food for a day."

"I warn you and your friends that I will shoot any of you at the first sign of aggression." He was straight up honest. That should make this easier.

"Understood," Zahra agreed.

The man Zahra had seen on the television the day before stepped out of the shadows of the open doorway. The rifle in his hand was not pointing at her, which she took as a good sign.

"How many people do you have?"

"Ten altogether, three women and seven men. Is it okay for them to come out now?"

"Yes, but I will protect the people here at any cost."

Zahra had to admit the human-shifter was brave and loyal, but that didn't erase all the pain and destruction humans had caused from her memory.

"What's your name?" Zahra asked.

"Trooper Ben Brown."

"Which state?" John asked as he joined Zahra.

"Texas."

"What's a Texas trooper doing in the British countryside?" Rose asked as she arrived with Riker and Xander.

"Damn work exchange bullshit. I should have been back stateside when all this went down."

Zahra noticed Ben's shiny badge in the shape of a star. Zahra wondered what the state trooper was going to do now that there wasn't an actual police force left.

"It wouldn't have made a difference. North America got hit as hard as everywhere else," John explained. "Did you have any family back home?"

"My mom, but she'd good at taking care of herself," Ben answered, and Zahra got the distinct impression there was more to that statement.

The remaining warriors joined them along with Marie, and if Zahra hadn't lost her senses, she was positive Ben's nostrils flared, resembling a shifter scenting the air. His dark brown eyes were locked on Marie until Zahra's friend stepped behind John and out of Ben's view. *Interesting.*

Before she had enough time to analyze their reaction to each other, the small girl Zahra had seen on the street that day limped up behind Ben and grabbed on to his leg.

"Ben, I'm hungry," the tot whispered while sneaking peeks at the new arrivals.

"When we found this place, it had been cleaned out for the winter, I was able to find blankets but no food. Also, Jenny here has a cut to her thigh, and I don't have any supplies or medicine. I was going to make a run for the town a couple miles down the road, but I didn't want to leave the kids alone."

A second head popped up in the front bay window. A boy with a mop of red hair, much like Ben's, who looked to be younger than the little girl. One of the warriors brought up a first aid bag and handed it to Ben.

"Thank you, I'm grateful," Ben said. "Come on in so I can look at Jenny's leg while they eat."

"Take up positions around the cottage in case we have company," John ordered his warriors before taking Zahra by the hand and leading her off to the side of the cottage. "Thank you for not going in there alone. I would have had to follow, and things would have turned out differently."

Zahra reached up and ran the palm of her hand over John's handsome jaw. *"You're welcome."* Then she lifted onto her toes, pulled down the mask, and kissed her mate's chin. She loved this man so much.

John huffed and shook his head. "You're going to be the reason I get gray hair."

"You'll look sexy as a silver-fox...or bear, as the case may be," Zahra teased, taking his hand and leading him into the now crowded cottage. Marie had chosen to remain outside.

The two children sat on an old flowered couch, munching away on granola bars and drinking bottles of water. Rose sat between them while Ben cleaned out the cut on Jenny's leg.

"This is Matthew. I found him hiding under a seat on one of those double-decker buses. He hasn't spoken since then, and the only reason I know his name is because he was wearing a nametag. I'm guessing he must have been on some school trip or something."

Zahra knelt in front of Matthew and fished out two peppermint candies she'd stashed in her pocket. She loved the taste of peppermint. She held one out to each of the children while the betas, John and Ben, discussed their next move.

Jenny took the candy and said, "Thank you."

Matthew, on the other hand, wasn't so quick to accept her offer. Instead, he reached out to touch the facemask Zahra was wearing. It became apparent that he didn't like not being able to see her entire face, so Zahra slid the ear straps off and removed it.

The little guy studied her carefully before smiling wide and taking the candy from her hand.

"Hello, Matthew, I'm happy to meet you too." Zahra smiled wide and was about to open the wrapper when Ben jumped to his feet.

"Your mouth didn't move when you spoke."

Shit. Zahra had forgotten for a split second.

"We have company," Marie yelled as she ran into the room. "Collector demons are moving in from across the pasture out back."

So much for breaking it to the trooper easily.

Shit was about to hit the fan.

Chapter Eleven

"We aren't the enemy," Zahra growled. *"If we wanted to, we could have easily taken you out, so I suggest you point that thing at the hosts coming, or my mate is going to go super-grizzly on your ass,"* Zahra warned while keeping a close eye on the rifle now in Ben's hands.

A strange emotion crossed his face, but it was gone before Zahra had a chance to figure it out. "Mate?" Ben said with a tinge of disbelief while looking around the room. "You're all shifters?"

"Oh shit," Rose said through their link. *"How does he know about shifters?"*

Several guns were now trained on the trooper, and Marie came straight out and asked, "Are you a hunter?" She looked devastated.

Rose had the children behind her, and out of the way in case someone went furry.

Ben's not-so-attractive scrunched-up nose made it look like the guy smelled something rotten. This wasn't boding well for this whole mission.

"Hunters are the dregs of mankind," Ben responded vehemently. "There isn't a hole deep enough to bury those assholes."

"Okay, now I'm confused," Zahra said, and by looking around, she wasn't alone.

A warrior ran through the front door. "Collector demons less than one hundred yards out."

"There's no time for this," John stated. "We need to get these kids out of here."

"Rose, you take everyone to safety, and John and I will hold them off as long as we can. We can't leave the other three warriors out there. Xander, I need you to watch over my mate for me." When it looked like Xander would argue. Riker continued, "The pack and clan need one of us to return immediately, or there'll be panic. Go."

"I'll be back for you, mate," Rose said as she took the children's hands.

Riker smiled, shifted into his bear, and ran out the front door.

"Go with Rose," John said before kissing Zahra. "I'll be back home in no time."

Zahra wanted to argue but knew it would do no good. John was the head of Porda Clan's warriors, and this was his duty. *"I'll be waiting."*

Soon, John was gone as had Riker, and Zahra was left staring at the empty doorway.

"Let's go," Marie said, snapping Zahra out of her shock.

"Wait a minute, go where…how? We're surrounded," Ben said. "I could try clearing a path for you, but it would have helped if those guys just hadn't taken off."

"We don't need to leave the cottage," Zahra explained. *"Simply hold out your hand."*

When he didn't move, Marie stepped in. "Get your hand out there now, trooper. We are about to teleport away from here."

"Teleport?" Ben asked, incredulous, as he inched closer to the children. Gunfire began to erupt from outside the cottage. Zahra's mind went to her mate, who was out there in the middle of that gunfire.

"We don't have time for this," Marie said seconds before bashing Ben over the head and knocking him unconscious. "He'll have a headache, but he'll be alive."

Xander picked up Ben, and the remaining joined hands along with the children. Rose's goddess markings glowed bright, and Zahra pulled her hand back out of Marie's reach at the last moment, then they were gone.

Zahra couldn't leave her mate and the others behind, or to have Rose risk herself coming back for them. *"If any one of you five Eyes could do me a favor, make sure that Rose can't teleport back here."* No one else needed to jeopardize their safety for her mission.

Zahra looked down at her now glowing hands and took that as a good sign. Her palms began to burn the same as when Sekhmet attacked her. The fact that Rose hadn't returned yet confirmed she'd been heard. Zahra wished she'd been given an instruction manual along with these powers. Teleportation should be simple, Rose and

Raz seemed to have picked it up quickly, so what the hell was wrong with her?

She didn't have much time to figure that out. The first host came through the door, and on instinct, Zahra raised her hand, pointing her palm at the demon and then…nothing. Nothing happened. *Shit.*

The host wore a toothy grin as he ambled into the living room. It was odd seeing them behaving so much like humans. Then it spoke.

"They leave you here all alone, lass?"

As what had to have been a middle-aged Scottish man at one point, dressed in a blue suit, circled around her, the pinky finger of his right hand fell off onto the ground. *Damn.*

"I see you haven't quite figured out how to keep your hosts in one piece," Zahra said in an attempt to distract him long enough for her to get a few more tries in with her hands. It had been so easy to use when Zahra had been faced with Sekhmet. What was she doing wrong?

Rubbing her palm on her shirt wasn't helping. Trying to picture a light flowing out of her didn't help either. *Why isn't this working?* She tried over and over again, getting angrier with each failure. By now, the demon's host was standing only a few feet away, laughing in a weird mix of cackle-cough. "Something wrong with your hands?"

Zahra could almost feel her blood boiling. She raised her palms at the death bringer and screamed, *"Fuck you."*

Light poured from her hands, disintegrating the demon into dust on contact. Another came through the door, and Zahra did the same. One after another was turned to dust as she worked her way out of the cottage, heading toward the pasture.

She couldn't help but notice that none of the demons had floated out of their host bodies when she'd turned them to dust. Usually, they would make a break for it so that they could infect someone else. Zahra would have to remember to mention that.

The sounds of fighting brought her deeper into the forest. Zahra knew she was creating enough light to ward off approaching spaceships. Her mate would know she was coming. She hoped the team would be together. It would be more difficult trying to find one at a time.

She felt a sting in her shoulder and looked down and confirmed it was only a graze from a bullet and carried on. As Zahra got closer to where the action was, she could see bears down on the ground while others carried on fighting in both forms. More bullets whistled by her, but there was no way she was stopping.

The hosts appeared to be thinning out, and Zahra made a run for the team. John was still standing, but Riker was on the ground, along with one other warrior. The second their gazes met, Zahra knew her mate was pissed. Too bad.

The other two warriors began backing up closer to the two downed men and John. *"Yes, that's perfect. I can teleport us out of here faster if you're together."*

A female host jumped onto John's back, and Zahra took aim, turning her to dust. Fortunately, she saw Riker's eyes open when John picked him up. He was still alive. Zahra took off at a run, holding her fingers out, reaching for her mate's outstretched hand.

The entire time she chanted one word repeatedly: home, home, home.

They touched, and Zahra felt her feet leave the forest floor. The world swirled around her, but never once did she stop chanting her destination, praying they didn't end up worse off than they were before.

Finally, her feet touched the ground, and she collapsed onto a carpeted floor. Zahra looked around, and sure enough, she'd gotten them back to the facility, more specifically one of the communal spaces where several bears were now standing.

Chaos ensued as people ran in to help the injured. Thankfully none were dead as far as she could tell. Jewel was busy assessing everyone, and Zahra stepped out of the way. In moments, the room was filled, and then soon after, Rose and Mason arrived, followed by Raz, Axel, and Xander.

After Rose had checked in with Riker, she stormed over to Zahra. *This doesn't look good.*

"How dare you do that to me and don't even try to deny it. I couldn't teleport back at the same time you let go of Marie's hand. You forced me to sit here and wait to see if my mate was dead instead of allowing me to help. You're not some lone wolf anymore. I'll never forgive you for taking away my choice." Rose's canines were extended, and she was growling as she spoke, gaining them a lot of attention.

Mason came over and wrapped his arms around Rose before leading her out of the room. Zahra didn't understand. She had been trying to protect them. She walked over to John, who was busy lifting one of his warriors onto the waiting gurney. The nail marks from the female host who'd jumped onto his back ran down both of his shoulders. They'd have to clean that thoroughly. Who knew what had been under her nails.

Zahra came to his side, but he wasn't quick to acknowledge her, so she placed her hand on his back. John turned, but the look of relief and happiness that she'd expected was not there. Instead, he looked angry and exhausted. He did take a moment to look her over, and when he was satisfied Zahra wasn't suffering any significant injuries, he went back to staring at her as if trying to make a decision.

"Are you okay, mate?" Zahra asked. She was beginning to get worried.

"Of course, I'm not okay," John answered abruptly, and in a voice she'd never heard before. "Why do you never listen to me? I said to come back here with Rose, where it was safe, but did you listen? Of course not. Then I see you running through a forest packed with hosts as if you were lighting it up for Christmas."

"But I can defend myself. You've seen me." Zahra wasn't sure what the problem was.

John shook his head and said, "Last time I checked, you hadn't had any control over your powers. I'm not sure this is going to work out. I have to check on my guys in the infirmary. We'll talk later."

Without even kissing her, John turned and followed the gurneys out of the room. Zahra looked around, stunned, and not quite sure what had happened.

Marie was walking her way, and Zahra panicked. She couldn't take another person telling her how big a disappointment she had been. Zahra zeroed in on a single thought and teleported away.

Chapter Twelve

It had been hours since John was cleaned up and released from the infirmary, but here he sat staring at a chart over the sink that spelled out the proper way to wash your hands to prevent the spread of disease and infection. He wasn't so sure they had to worry about those things considering they were shifters, but it was useful information to have now that they had humans among them.

Trooper Ben had been restricted to his room until everyone could recover from the events of the day. The two children had been given their own room with their own private nanny of sorts. Hope had volunteered for the job, and rumor had it she'd been seen giving the two bear rides up and down the halls. Apparently, the kids loved it, and neither had shown any fear of the animals roaming around the facility. Which was good considering this was their new home for the foreseeable future.

One of his warriors was forced to remain in the infirmary overnight, but other than that, Riker had been released to rest with his family, and the other two warriors were treated for minor injuries and sent home. The scratches and lacerations he'd sustained had been cleaned twice and were already healing. He'd waited for Zahra to come to have her wounds checked, even though John had determined none were severe, but his mate hadn't shown up.

He thought about returning to their room, but after what he'd said and done, he wasn't sure of the reception he'd get, or if she even wanted him there. Nothing had come through their private link since the hurt he had felt from her when he'd walked away.

He had been angry and terrified by his mate's actions. With no thought of her own safety, she'd run out into the middle of danger. She'd proven that repeatedly. His mate was impulsive, headstrong, reckless, brave, loving, kind, protective, and capable. He was angry and proud at the same time, but worry won out over it all. He could have lost her, and she didn't seem to realize the jeopardy she put herself in.

He wasn't entirely sure what came over him when they'd made it back to the communal room. Even after witnessing Rose tear a strip off Zahra, he'd basically done the same thing, but worse. He'd betrayed their bond and his oath to always stand by her side. How could she forgive them? Hell, he hadn't even kissed her before walking away: the woman who'd saved his life repeatedly. What was wrong with him?

"So, you're in the doghouse too?" Rose asked from the open doorway leading out into the hall.

"At least you had an honest issue. Fuck, I yelled at her because she saved my life. I don't even know how it got that far out of control. Sure, I was upset by her risking her life, and I was scared for her safety, but my reaction was way out of hand."

Rose huffed and walked into the infirmary, sitting down in the chair opposite his. "Honest issue. Yeah, right. I was terrified when I saw Riker covered in blood. I needed someone to blame, and I guess since there wasn't a demon around I could kill, I went after Zahra when in truth, she'd been protecting me as she always does.

"Who knows what would have happened if she had come back to wait here. Would we all be dead? Would I have been able to reach the team when I came back? By the sounds of things, Zahra was putting up one hell of a fight even with her powers. Who's to say I could have made it through that and rescued the five of you?"

"We have a serious amount of apologizing to do," John agreed.

"So, you have to go out, find her, and bring her back," Rose said.

"Find her? Why would I need to find her? Isn't she in our room?" This couldn't be good.

"No, Marie told me after you left, Zahra vanished, and no one has seen her since."

John's stomach dropped. He stood and was about to go check their room when Jewel came in from her office. "Ah, there you are. I need to talk to you about something I've found."

No way was John stopping to have a discussion. He had to find his mate. "It'll have to wait. I've got to talk with Zahra."

"Yes, I've heard about your previous talk when all of you returned, and what I've found might pertain to it," Jewel explained, but she didn't look thrilled with him, and he couldn't blame her.

"How?"

"The scratches on your shoulders from the host's fingernails seem to have had a living bacteria of sorts under them. I assume from the host. When I first cleaned your wounds, I noticed the strange substances and took a sample to test. Then we cleaned your wound the second time, and I was able to confirm all the bacteria had been killed."

"Why didn't you tell me when you found it?" John asked.

"The mood you were in when you arrived here was scary enough to keep a few of my nurses away. No way would you have sat down for a conversation."

"I wasn't that bad, was I?" John's stomach was churning.

Jewel nodded. "However, now I may have a cause for that, and if so, we need to figure out how to prevent it from affecting more shifters."

"What did you find?" Rose asked.

Jewel opened the screen on her tablet and showed them test results. "The bacteria under the host's nails seem to have microbes that can travel to the brain and are responsible for increases in testosterone."

"Okay, but my body and brain are already used to having testosterone around." John didn't understand.

"Yes, of course, but the amounts these microbes produce are extremely high. Testosterone is an androgen. You find increased androgen in athletes using steroids. In humans, it can cause something called 'roid rage,'" Jewel explained, and things were now becoming clearer. The chemicals humans intentionally put into their bodies boggled the mind.

Rose stood up and joined them. "So what you're saying is since John was scratched by that host, it increased his aggression and anger. Which may have made him more aggressive toward Zahra for risking her life."

"In essence, yes. I'll have to do more testing because this could be a real problem for shifters," Jewel stated while flipping through a few more screens.

"What do you mean?" John asked. Knowledge helped them be ready for anything.

"If the hosts are carrying these microbes and they can somehow get it into a shifter's system, depending on the levels, it could send one of our kind into a blind rage. Subsequently making it easier for hosts to kill us because the shifter wouldn't be able to think logically until it's flushed from their system."

Well shit.

"Shit," Rose echoed. "Do you believe this is being done on purpose or simply a side effect of the demons taking a host?"

"If we can't figure out a way to vaccinate for it or create an antidote, it's a non-issue," Jewel said. "I can't be sure yet if this is intentional, but you might actually consider this to be fortunate. Since we found this microbe so early on in this fight, we have a chance of making it extinct quickly before the numbers affected become too high."

"It makes sense. Once you'd cleaned out my wounds, I began to feel calmer, and the realization hit about what I'd said to my mate." John really had to find Zahra.

"Is that why you've been hiding out here?" Jewel asked.

John glanced side to side to make sure they were alone. "Yeah, I deserve to have my ass kicked for what I did. Of course, I was upset that my mate could have been hurt, but nothing compared to when we were standing in that room. The rage I felt took over all my thoughts and seemed to justify my actions even as my instincts told me to stop. That lack of control over my actions is terrifying."

"I'll let my mates know what's going on," Rose said. "At least now we may have a cause for your anger toward Zahra. Me, I'm still a bitch."

John couldn't help but smile. "Somehow, I think Zahra will forgive you anyway."

"Well, you better figure out where she is," Rose commented.

"I think I have an idea."

***

Zahra watched the fluffy white clouds drift overhead. Each one unique, like a snowflake, like a waterfall, and like her. She was unique, too unique to be around, but still unique. So at least that had proven her former matriarch wrong. She wasn't a nothing, she was…what was she, really?

Rolling over onto her four feet, she dug her claws into the damp earth. Another bright sunny morning, the birds were singing, the breeze had cooled as fall took hold, and Zahra was as lost as ever. Well, maybe not physically, because she was standing beside her parents' grave, but emotionally she might as well be off drifting in the middle of the ocean.

She took a deep breath and let it out slowly before padding into the forest toward the stream. One thing she didn't miss from before was all the collector demon hosts. Usually, being out here in the bush didn't seem to attract much of their attention, which she didn't mind in the least.

The stream was frosty this early in the morning, but she'd lived many years through worse, so she shoved her discomfort aside and waded in. The first few licks were frigid, but it would do. At least the stream moved fast enough so as not to freeze in winter.

She'd already begun building her den to survive the winter, and if she tried really hard, she could almost feel like she'd never left. That she never had a fated mate or friends. There was no happy ending, no matter how much she wished it or missed it.

"Oh, boohoo. Seriously, grow some balls, puppy."

Zahra didn't even bother to respond. She'd sensed Sekhmet long before she decided to appear. Another few licks and Zahra stepped out of the water, ignored the lioness lounging on the rocks, and headed for her den.

Peace had been hard to come by since the annoying goddess had shown, and no matter how hard she'd tried to ignore her, Sekhmet kept cropping up. Hadn't she been punished enough? Some Eye of Ra she turned out to be.

"Apparently not," Sekhmet chimed in as she followed Zahra through the forest.

Zahra stopped and shook out her thick coat, sending droplets of water flying in Sekhmet's direction. The majestic cat growled and whined her anger at having a slight shower. Zahra huffed her laughter and carried on.

"Poor kitty. Is the lioness not used to the cold temperatures of the Pacific Northwest? Not a hot savannah in sight."

"I will gut you, dog," Sekhmet threatened as she licked her coat clean.

Sadly, Zahra actually wished the lioness would do it. But alas, she was all growl and no bite. It had been twelve days since she'd left the Porda Clan and her mate. No one had come to check on her, and she couldn't connect with the link any longer. It was painfully apparent that between the problems she'd caused John and the stunt she'd pulled on Rose, she'd been banished. She could handle the banishment, but the separation from her mate left her lost and broken.

"Oh come on. You're going to throw away everything you've been given because a male saw you as a problem?"

"That male is my fated mate."

"So?"

"Says the goddess who obviously never had one."

"I wouldn't be too sure of that."

Zahra stopped outside her den. She'd been building it in a small cave she'd used numerous times over the years before meeting the Porda Clan and John. She'd brought in new branches and leaves in hopes of making it warmer than it had been in the last few years when she'd given up altogether and hadn't bothered fixing it.

"You have a mate?"

"As a matter of fact, I do."

"Then why aren't you home bothering him?"

"I would be if you got your issues dealt with."

Zahra was done trying to figure the crazy cat out and crawled into her den instead of answering. The cave was small, but it would be easier to keep warm. Her mind wandered to the warmth she'd felt when surrounded by her big bear. Her wolf let out a low whine of pain at the memory. What she'd do to be in those arms again.

"Yes, do tell. What would you do?"

"Will you stay out of my head?" All she wanted was peace. Instead, she got a pain-in-the-ass lioness shadow.

Zahra curled into a ball amongst her leaves and twigs and tried to block out the migraine named Sekhmet. Wasn't the constant pain she was in enough of a penance?

"Would you forget your past and everything you've been through?" Sekhmet asked as she squeezed her lioness body into the den.

"How could I?"

"Would you return your gifts and allow the past to play out as fated?"

Zahra refused to answer. It wasn't even a question. Of course, she'd keep her gifts if it meant Asta and those other shifters were alive.

"Shifters? Some humans are alive because of you as well."

"What difference does it make?"

"All the difference in the world. How do you know if Jenny or Matthew are meant to be the first shifter president?"

Zahra's head flew up and bashed off the ceiling of the cave. Of course, making the lioness huff in laughter.

"They aren't shifters."

"You don't know that, and you don't know the future. So, would you have changed the events of that night? Never finding Trooper Ben, or Jenny and Matthew? They'd be left in that cottage for the hosts to find."

Zahra was starting to get pissed. When would enough be enough?

"Chosen by Ra himself, only to be defeated by your mate's scolding? I honestly thought you were a stronger female than that. The first thing you do is run away, instead of facing the problem and standing up for yourself. You are disappointing, wolfie."

Zahra was fuming. She'd given everything of herself to others. She'd been tortured and hunted, abandoned and alone, yet she carried on. She'd fought the collector demons and saved lives. How dare this spoiled goddess call her disappointing? The growl ripped from her throat was Sekhmet's only warning before Zahra charged forward. The lioness bolted from the den and headed straight into the forest. Zahra gave chase. Everything she'd done and been through boiled below the surface and demanded its due.

She wasn't a nothing, she wasn't a disappointment, and she wasn't a failure. She was strong, she was a warrior, and she deserved to be loved for her abilities and faults. To make her own choices, to rush into battle like any other warrior and not be concerned who she pissed off.

But most of all, she deserved respect from herself and from others.

"Finally," Sekhmet growled before the lioness Zahra had been chasing vanished, and the world around her shifted, bringing her smack-dab into the middle of the clan house.

It took her a moment to register what she was seeing before skidding to a stop short of slamming her head into one of the fireplaces in the now-empty great room.

"What's going on?"

"Come on, isn't it obvious?" Sekhmet asked in her human form.

"Humor me."

"You've been returned to the Porda Clan house."

"Yes, I'm aware of that, but why?"

"Because your mate is nearby. He's been searching for you since you left."

"Really, I'd think my parents' grave would have been an obvious first choice," Zahra growled. *"What are you playing at? If John wanted to find me, that would have been the first place he'd look."*

For the first time since she arrived, Sekhmet wasn't so confident. She bit her lip and looked everywhere but into Zahra's eyes. *"What did you do?"*

"It wasn't me," Sekhmet quickly pointed out. "Ra was less than impressed with your poor-me, run-away attitude, so he made it impossible for anyone to find you until you figured out your true worth and what it was you deserved."

"How?" Zahra had a sinking feeling she already knew.

"Well, first, he severed your link to the clan and your mate."

"I thought I'd been banished."

"Yeah, not so much," Sekhmet admitted. "When John or a search party got close to your location, Ra led them in another direction or made it seem as if you weren't there."

"All this time, I thought no one wanted me."

"Here's the thing, shit like that right there is why Ra did it. 'No one wants me' and 'you're too much trouble.' On and on with this nagging doubt. Now is not the time for doubt. People will look up to you in times of crisis, and the last thing they need is to find a self-doubting goddess who runs at a few angry words."

"I'd never seen John like that."

"Maybe there's a reason for his behavior. How would you know since you didn't stick around to find out?" Sekhmet had a point, which pissed Zahra off even further. "Look, I understand how much it hurt to be the target of their anger. On top of that, you've been through so much in your life. I respect your strength and the courage it took to live through that, but you're no longer that girl in the pit.

Of course, you'll never forget it, but you can't let it rule your life anymore."

Zahra was caught off guard. Sekhmet respected her, wow.

"Don't let it go to your head."

People would look to her for strength. What kind of person did she want them to find? Not the one cowering by a gravesite, or second-guessing every decision she made. Zahra wanted to be everything they needed: strong, loyal, ethical, compassionate, and unafraid to stand up for herself, and to give them a sense of peace and strength.

"I get it now."

"Well, it's about time," Sekhmet said while making exaggerated hand signs above her head in the shape of her head blowing up. Weird. "Now, whatcha going to do about it?"

Zahra didn't even need to think about it. *"Thank you, Sekhmet."* She pictured precisely where she wanted to be most, and with a smile, she vanished.

Chapter Thirteen

John sat in the boardroom, going over new reports sent in from the last team sent out to search for any sign of his mate. Every day he repeated the same routine: perform his duties as general, then search for Zahra. Those were the only things necessary for him to keep breathing. His duties kept him sane through it all, and searching kept his hopes up that they'd find her.

Jewel and Doc Hanley had come up with a vaccine to counteract the effects of the host's bacteria. The only drawback was anyone having to go to the surface had to get a booster shot each and every time. Personally, John had never been fond of needles.

The human-shifter and two children, Jenny and Matthew, had acclimated well to their new surroundings. Although Jenny continued to have nightmares, and Matthew hadn't spoken yet, they were doing better than expected.

Many shifters traveled these halls in multiple forms, yet neither child seemed overly concerned about it. John figured that compared to what they'd seen outside, as long as the people and animals in here were friendly, the kids were okay. There were a few shifters who avoided the human children, but overall most accepted that they were living among them.

Trooper Ben still hadn't explained how he'd known about shifters, and with all the other concerns they had to deal with, no one had pressured him. He had to know the time would come for an explanation, but until then, Ben wouldn't be told why he was rescued along with the children. First, Ben needed to gain the trust of the shifters in this facility before any information would be shared.

Of course, they allowed him to watch the reports on what was happening aboveground. He had the right to know what they faced the same as everyone else. Ben spent most of his time searching for any information on a small town outside Dallas, Texas, named

Clarksville. John wondered if that had been where the officer was stationed or perhaps where his family was.

Hope continued to care for Jenny and Matthew. She had become attached to them, even issuing the occasional growl if someone got too rough playing with them or was known to hate humans to the extent they couldn't be trusted around the children even with the triads' explicit command that they not be touched.

John couldn't help but wonder how that situation would turn out. In truth, he'd tried to distract himself from his own pain by keeping tabs on the new arrivals, instead of fixating on what he'd done to drive his mate away.

Sure, he could blame it on the host bacteria, but that only intensified anger he already had in him. He realized he gave orders and expected them to be followed. It was the general in him. But when Zahra came along, things changed. She didn't *have to* listen to him.

John had been raised and trained for his one position: General of Warriors for the Porda Clan. His dad was the general before him, and so was his granddad. With shifters, there were certain positions that you could be born into, and John had been destined to become a general. The man who was responsible for the lives and deaths of the warriors beneath him and the clan he'd sworn to protect with his life.

To ensure that safety, he had to always be in control, ready for anything on a moment's notice. With his mate, he found out too late that the same attitude wasn't going to work. Zahra was strong and capable, hell, more capable than most with extraordinary abilities to protect herself and others. His overbearing nature had to be reined in.

Rose and Raz had tried reaching out to Zahra without any luck. They were completely cut off, and the kicker of it all was somehow learning someone else was controlling it. A god had severed their link, and he wondered if Ra, the sun god who'd chosen Zahra as an Eye, was involved somehow.

It all was coming to a head. John hadn't been eating properly or sleeping, and the stubble on his face was beginning to look suspiciously like a beard. He was falling apart without his mate, and he'd been the one who'd driven her away.

He threw the latest report back onto the boardroom table and rubbed his tired, sore eyes. He didn't even want to think about Zahra not coming back, because then he'd have no hope at all left.

The first trickle of awareness flowed through his private link and into his heart. John stilled to confirm that he hadn't imagined it. Sure enough within moments, he felt it again, and even more exciting, he could sense where it was coming from.

Jumping up out of his chair, he startled the others in the room. Both alphas looked at him with concern from the other end of the table. Rose seemed as excited as he was. She must have felt it too.

"Is everything all right?" Mason asked while setting his tablet down in front of him.

"Yes," John answered. "Better than it has been in days. Zahra's here." Then he took off out the office door and down the long corridor leading to the main staircases on the east side of the facility.

Without breaking stride, he took the stairs two at a time. People rushed to get out of his way as he raced past them. Level after level, he ran until he stood outside his and Zahra's private room. His mate was in there, and he didn't know if he should knock or rush in.

"Get in here." Zahra's voice traveled through his mind, comforting him. He'd missed this intimacy so much.

He reached for the door handle but wasn't fast enough as the door flew open, and Zahra jumped up into his arms. John's heart felt like it was going to explode, but he was able to keep his wits about him and carried his mate inside their room. The feel of her back in his arms, holding him, kissing the side of his neck, was almost too much for his exhausted mind to process.

"I've missed you so much," he began. "I'm sorry for what I said and how I treated you. This is all my fault. I'll do whatever it takes to make this up to you."

"I'm sorry I ran away. I honestly believed I wasn't wanted. Then when no one came—"

"I searched, we sent out teams," John assured her. "I would have looked for you forever."

Zahra nodded her head in understanding. *"Ra is responsible for that along with severing our link. I thought I'd been banished. Rose was furious with me, and then when you said you didn't think we were going to work out, I panicked."*

"I have so much to explain and apologize for," he said as he sat on the couch while keeping Zahra in his arms. He wasn't sure if he'd be able to let go of his mate anytime soon. "I should have never said those things."

Zahra looked up at him, her eyes wet with tears. *"Why did you?"*

"I admit that I was upset and afraid for you, and yes, angry, but not as hostile as I appeared to be. This is not an excuse for my behavior, but Jewel discovered a bacteria in the scratches left on my shoulders from the host who jumped onto my back. She ran multiple tests and determined that the bacteria increases a person's testosterone level to the point of inexplicable rage. Jewel and Doc Hanley were able to come up with a vaccine for now."

"Show me please," Zahra asked.

John opened his mind to her, but not merely regarding the bacteria. He shared every moment since she'd left, from his guilt and regret to the searches and every failed attempt to find her, including his sleepless nights and long days piling up until he struggled to carry on.

In response, Zahra did the same. He saw how cruel he'd appeared through her eyes when he'd confronted her about not doing what he said, and his vicious comment about this not working out. Honestly, he didn't even know where those words came from. John didn't even recognize himself, making it more apparent why she'd looked so stunned.

Sekhmet had been with his mate the entire time, and John could see why Zahra considered the goddess to be a pain in the ass. However, the fact that Sekhmet didn't leave Zahra alone in the forest was enough to make him wonder if the goddess actually cared on some level. Ra's part in this quickly became apparent, as well as the reasons why the god felt it necessary to intervene.

John was floored to realize that he'd missed the fact that Zahra was struggling with her worth and place in the clan, and he hadn't helped with his overbearing behavior.

"I'm sorry, love."

"So am I," she replied. *"I'm not innocent in all of this. Since coming to the Porda Clan, I've been ready to return back to my forest at a moment's notice."* Zahra cuddled deeper into John's arms. *"How can I say I tried to accept my life in the clan and as your mate when I was already prepared to leave it behind?"*

"It wasn't as if I helped with your worry. Instead of assuring you of your place here, especially after what you'd been through, I assumed everything would fall into place. I should have trusted in you more, in your powers and capabilities. You have every right to make your own decisions, and I respect you and everything you've done surviving on your own."

"I think I've known that since the beginning, but somehow it all got twisted in my mind. I love you, and I never want to be away from you again. If anything, I've learned more about myself in the time that I've known you, than at any other time in my life."

"Don't worry about being away from me ever again. I don't think I'm going to let you out of my arms for a while. I've missed you, my love. This old bear is lost without you."

Zahra smiled wide before running her fingers through his unintentional beard. *"I see you're trying a new look. Hairy in and out of shifted form."*

"Smart-ass. God, I've missed you," John admitted while holding her closer.

"You look exhausted," she stated while scratching his hairy chin, which felt so good. *"Do you have time for a shower? I could shave this for you, and maybe we could both get a decent amount of sleep. My den was a failure."*

"I have all the time in the world for you, mate. I'm sure by now, everyone knows you're back, and someone will step up while we have our time together." He would enjoy his beautiful mate and never take anything for granted.

"Good, because I have plans for you, my big bear."

***

"So, I'm happy to see that you've returned, Zahra."

She turned away from the television screen to look at her old friend. Rose had been avoiding her since she'd returned from the forest. Though John had assured her that Rose hadn't meant what she'd said, Zahra still wasn't sure.

"Hello, Rose," Zahra said. *"I'm happy to be here."*

Damn, this was painfully awkward. Not even after being separated over fifty years had their reunion been this stress-filled.

Rose walked over to the couch Zahra was sitting on. "May I join you?"

"Of course." Yep, awkward.

"Have you gotten enough rest since your return?" Rose asked. "John has looked much healthier over the last couple of days."

"Yes, I'm feeling well." Physically.

Zahra was terrified that this was their relationship now. A strained conversation about mundane stuff. Would they never be able to get the friendship they shared back?

"Okay, this sucks. I can't stand that we aren't talking," Rose said as she reached out and took Zahra's hand. "I'm a bitch, and I'm sorry for what I said to you. I blamed you for Riker being hurt when the truth is you saved his life. Taking my fear and anger out on you wasn't cool. I'm embarrassed by my actions, and I hope you can forgive me."

Zahra sucked in a deep breath, slid over on the couch, and took her friend in a big hug. This was Rose, her friend. The one who couldn't help but take care of everyone she met. Even when Rose was in the pit, she managed to care about the children sneaking her food. Worried they'd get caught and punished for giving her a few pieces of dried meat or bread.

Everyone had times they regret, words said in haste and fear when they couldn't see past their own pain. Rose was a kind, loving person and friend, and a few angry words said at a stressful time would never be reason enough to lose that friendship.

Zahra released Rose from their hug and asked, *"So want to go see what Hope and the kids are up to?"*

Rose smiled slowly and brushed away a tear before saying, "I would love to."

Enjoy this sneak peek at the fourth book in the Fated Mates series:

Merciless

Marie knew what she was doing was wrong. She'd try to talk herself out of it, force herself to see reason, anything to stop her from sitting exactly where she currently was. It was no surprise when her heart rate sped up. It always happened that way. Her palms were sweaty, and she rubbed them on her jeans before turning the page on a book she wasn't even reading.

Her water bottle was already empty, and there were at least thirty minutes left if he stayed on the same routine. Marie didn't want to risk running to fill up her bottle, not wanting to miss anything. She wasn't the only one who came here, but she was the only one with a legitimate reason. She'd been assigned to do this, sit and watch.

Muscles flexed and strained under the weight being lifted, but they never faltered. Beads of sweat rolled down miles of delicious tanned skin, making her almost moan at the sight. She knew from the moment she set her eyes on the guy that she'd be in a whole new world of trouble, and maybe this time, Rose won't be able to save her.

But did she look away? Of course not.

Instead, every day from ten in the morning until noon, she sat spellbound while trying to appear unaffected while Texas State Trooper Ben Brown worked out in the large, fully equipped gym installed on the tenth level.

Of course, they required an extensive gym, plus-sized, for shifters trapped underneath the ground and unable to go for a run to burn off any pent-up energy or aggression. They were bears after all. Aggression was in their DNA.

The human-shifter seemed to enjoy the benefits of a good workout, and so did Marie for entirely different reasons.

Off to the left side of the area, she noticed two female wolf shifters were scanning the room. One shook her head and waved off whatever the other wolf had said before leaving the gym. The one who remained removed her t-shirt, leaving her standing there in her sports bra. It didn't take much to figure out what she had in mind.

Marie watched as a she-wolf shifter stepped onto an elliptical machine directly in front of where Ben was busy doing leg presses. Whatever the she-wolf was wearing didn't cover much To shifters, nudity wasn't a big deal, but Ben was human...mainly, so the woman might as well have been wearing a sign on her barely covered ass, declaring herself available.

Marie almost groaned aloud when the wolf's ass cheeks bounced from under her miniscule shorts. Seriously, that's how you went about attracting a man? If so, Marie was destined to be alone because there was no way in a million years she'd wear that.

Ben didn't even appear to notice the bouncy woman and moved on to the dumbbells. Marie had to give the woman credit: she wasn't easily deterred. Instead, she decided to move over to the treadmill across from the mirror Ben was using to check his form. Marie was positive that his form was on point.

She flipped another unread page with a bit more force than necessary, ripping the page out of the book in the process, and looked again at her empty water bottle. It didn't matter how thirsty she was, Marie wasn't going anywhere. When the wolf lowered the zipper on the front of her sports bra, Marie was surprised her breasts didn't fall out, causing her bear to growl and paw at her to do something.

The display reconfirmed that if this was what it took to get a male's attention, Marie didn't want it. She was a bear shifter, which made her taller and more substantial than a lot of other female shifter species. She had defined muscle and long legs. Her breasts weren't voluptuous, but they were nice, she thought. However, no matter what she did, Marie would never be a soft and curvy woman. She wasn't built that way.

Before she could get any further into her unflattering body comparisons, the she-wolf, who was busy adjusting her bra strap, didn't notice her bottle of water teetering on the edge of the handrail. Within a few seconds, the bottle fell onto the treadmill, making the woman misstep and go flying off the end of the treadmill like a torpedo launch from a submarine. She actually went through the air because she had the treadmill set way too high.

Marie couldn't help but laugh, but it soon faded when Ben went over to help the woman to her feet. When Ben tried to pull his hand back, the wolf refused to let it go as she smiled coyly and brushed her breasts up against Ben's muscled and tattooed arm.

Disgusted, Marie was about to look away when a new problem walked in, a male wolf shifter who didn't appear to be so happy about what he saw. Marie was up and out of her chair, intending to head off the disaster that was about to happen. By the time she made it over to Ben's side, an argument had already erupted, and by the look on the she-wolf's face, the attention was exactly what she wanted.

"How dare you touch one of our women," the male bellowed and puffed out his chest like a damn peacock.

"You should know women aren't property. Besides, I was only helping her up after she fell," Ben stated calmly. "Now, if you'll excuse me, I'll return to my workout."

Ben turned back to the rack of dumbbells, and Marie could have predicted what happened next. As the she-wolf's smile widened, the male wolf shifter raised his arm to sucker punch Ben in the back of his head. Before he could get off a blow, Marie reached out, grabbed the male wolf's arm, and flipped him over her back and onto the floor. Ben turned around at the same time Marie jammed her elbow into the wolf's jaw, ending the guy's attempts at getting back up.

There were benefits to being a bear shifter. One was being stronger than most other shifters. Unfortunately, there were also drawbacks, and the way Ben was looking at her in that moment was one of them. She wasn't dainty or delicate. She was a bear, and no matter what, she'd always be one.

"Time to go," Marie said to Ben before turning to the two interlopers on her usually fun Ben workout day. "You two know the leaders' decision, the humans are not to be touched. Now leave, or I will be forced to report you to the alpha triad."

"Humans are bloodthirsty killers. It makes sense a traitor like you would protect them." Sure, the nasty comment hurt—every time she heard one, they hurt—but now wasn't the time to show their effect on her.

"And you're the poster boy for proper puppy weekly. Now leave," Marie ordered while extending her six-inch claws for good measure, "before I change my mind and show you the door personally."

Marie glanced over at Ben as the wolves began walking away, to find him staring at her hands.

Her heart fell, and she retracted her claws.

Yep, she was not soft and delicate.

She was a bear.

ABOUT THE AUTHOR

Lilli Carlisle lives outside Toronto, Canada. She's a member of the Romance Writers of America and its chapter, Toronto Romance Writers. Lilli is a mother of two wonderful girls, wife to an amazing man, and servant to the pets in her life. Lilli writes contemporary and paranormal romance, and believes love should be celebrated and shared. After all, everybody needs a little romance, excitement, intrigue, and passion in their lives.

Connect with Lilli:
Instagram:/lillicarlisle
facebook.com/lillicarlisleauthor
twitter.com/LilliCarlisle

www.BOROUGHSPUBLISHINGGROUP.com

If you enjoyed this book, please write a review. Our authors appreciate the feedback, and it helps future readers find books they love. We welcome your comments and invite you to send them to info@boroughspublishinggroup.com. Follow us on Facebook, Twitter and Instagram, and be sure to sign up for our newsletter for surprises and new releases from your favorite authors.

Are you an aspiring writer? Check out www.boroughspublishinggroup.com/submit and see if we can help you make your dreams come true.

www.ingramcontent.com/pod-product-compliance
Lightning Source LLC
Chambersburg PA
CBHW020319130626
46549CB00003B/926